Happy, Sad, Funny, Mad

Stories

by

Scott William Foley

Titles and Years Published

<u>Happy</u>

A Pact Upheld (2007)

Game (2019)

George Winthrop Jr. Park (2009)

Why We Won (2013)

Cold Turkey (2008)

Depths (2019)

The Easter Egg Escapade (2009)

Drive By (2020)

The Back Pew (2008)

A Man Out Of Time (2011)

A Christmas Confrontation (2009)

<u>Sad</u>

Faces Unknown (2008)

Pacified (2019)

The Miscarried (2017)

Stranglehold (2020)

Promise (2019)

Chubby Tummy (2018)

Crisis (2020)

Together (2017)

<u>Funny</u>

A Blind Date for a New Year (2008)

A Man, His Wife, and His Comics (2017)

Healthy Balls (2017)

Over My Dead Body (2008)

Follow Me (2007)

Lovebirds (2009)

In This (2020)

Gunsmoke's All-In (2020)

Huffy (2020)

<u>Mad</u>

Actual Reality (2020)

Swingin the Clown (2017)

Natural Law (2020)

Road Rage (2017)

The One True (2017)

Terminal Synchronicity (2017)

Thumb War (2018)

The Echo Of Laughter (2018)

Besieged (2019)

Fallen Man (2019)

Phasks™ (2017)

Cornered (2019)

HAPPY

A Pact Upheld

When Heath Saylor opened the door to his home, he saw a man he hadn't thought about in thirty-seven years, and his heart filled with cold dread.

"Doyle Fye," Heath said, his voice petrified wood.

"Heath Saylor; I've found you," Doyle returned with a grin on his face.

They shook hands, one of them clammy like a slug caught in a rainstorm, the other's dry as Death Valley.

Doyle looked past Heath's shoulder into his home and commented, "You seem to be doing well."

There it is, Heath thought. *All the proof I need.*

"Aren't you going to ask me in?" Doyle asked.

After a moment's hesitation, Heath said, "Of course, yes. Please, come in."

Heath looked Doyle over as the taller man entered his sanctuary. Doyle wore simple blue jeans with a simpler white tee shirt under a pale green windbreaker sporting a stylized FDP on the back. He had a duffle bag with the same logo upon it slung over his shoulder. Contrasted with Heath's customary casual wear of khaki pants and a collared shirt, Doyle looked like he was getting ready for yard work.

"Can I offer you a drink?" Heath asked while rubbing his palms together.

"Soda of any sort, so long as it has caffeine, would be great," Doyle chuckled.

"Be right back. Just have a seat on the couch," Heath muttered before he slipped through a door and into the kitchen. There sat Elsie, his wife, at a table writing thank-you notes.

"Do we have company?" she asked without looking up.

"Indeed."

She heard the trepidation in her husband's voice and gave him her full attention. She watched as he yanked a glass from the cupboard and filled it with frigid tap water. As he stared out the window above the kitchen sink, the glass quickly overflowed. She grew alarmed when he didn't notice.

"Heath," she slowly began, "*who* is it?"

Finally tearing his gaze from the window, Elsie shuddered when her husband's blue eyes seemed a shade paler. He said, "A mistake."

She started to rise from her seat, but he pointed at her with his shaking finger, whispering, "I won't let him get away with it. He *won't* take our money. Stay put." He gulped down his water, then added, "Trust me."

Heath opened the refrigerator, withdrew a can of soda, and left the kitchen.

"I was starting to think you ran out the back door," Doyle laughed.

"No," Heath responded as he plopped down into his recliner. "Just telling my wife about you."

"Do I get to meet her?"

"She's not feeling well," Heath lied. "Perhaps another time."

"Sure," Doyle said, nodding his head and frowning a bit. "Well, we should get down to business."

"Listen, Doyle, I know why you're here, but we were just kids back then. We shouldn't take what was said too seriously."

"Are you *kidding* me?" Doyle asked, stunned.

Heath swallowed hard before he said, "We were drunk, Doyle. That was the last time I saw you. I honestly thought you'd forgotten about the whole thing."

Doyle held his palms up as he leaned forward on the flowered couch and confessed, "Hey, look, Heath, I know I've been a bad friend. I should have kept in touch. But listen, we made a pact, and I think it needs to be upheld."

"I didn't even see you at graduation, Doyle!" Heath yelled from the recliner across the room. He didn't want to get too close. "You disappeared! Now you show up and want to keep a promise made decades ago?"

Doyle seemed discomforted by Heath's building agitation and returned, "I couldn't waste time with graduation, Heath. That pact gave me the guts to get out there and try to make my dreams come true. I'm sorry, okay? I should have sent a postcard or something, but we'd been best friends for ten years by then! I thought you'd understand."

"And now you're here to throw my life into turmoil," Heath groaned. "Great."

At a loss, Doyle remarked, "Honestly, I thought you'd be a bit more excited about this."

Yeah, I can't wait to hand over half my life's savings, you jerk, Heath thought to himself. *I've worked my whole life for this house, and now I won't be able to make the payments on it anymore because of you.*

Heath simply stared at him without saying a word, his lips quivering, and so Doyle continued, "Well, anyway." He lifted his duffle bag and placed it on the coffee table before him. He unzipped it.

What? Do you think I have stacks of hundred-dollar bills in the next room, ready to dive into your ratty bag?

"We made a deal thirty-seven years ago, Heath, that—no matter what—if one of us struck it rich, we'd share half the profits with the other. We were both scared to death of graduating and ending up in the gutters, so the pact was supposed to give us courage to forge ahead, knowing no matter how rough life became, we could count on each other for a nice retirement. I intend for us to uphold that pact."

Doyle reached into the duffle bag, dug around a bit, then pulled out a check. He handed it over to Heath.

His hand now shaking for completely different reasons, Heath took the check and thought his eyes would roll across the floor when he saw the amount made out to him. The FDP logo was also on the check, as well as what it stood for.

"Fye Data Processing," Heath read.

"I got worried in the beginning when things weren't taking off here, but our agreement reassured me to keep trying. I went overseas and, well, things worked out pretty good over there."

Doyle stood up, walked over to Heath who remained seated, and stretched out his hand. When Heath finally took his eyes off the check and saw what his old friend intended, they shook.

Before he left, Doyle said, "Hey buddy, if you don't mind a suggestion, why don't you get yourself a nice mansion out in the country? Your nerves seem shot."

Game

When he saw the boot prints in the snow, he dove to his belly. There shouldn't be anyone near this land—not for at least three miles.

Holding his breath, he surveyed the area. They possibly already sighted him. The slightest movement or even a puff of his breath could betray his position.

If they were to kill him, they could poach those woods without fear of ever being discovered. That worked both ways, though. If he caught them, they'd never be seen or heard from again.

A few minutes passed in silence. Not even a breeze rustled the limbs. Finally, he exhaled. A fine mist floated away. He expected to be shot within seconds.

Nothing happened.

The forest spared him.

Darkness would ruin the day within a few hours, and he still had to trek a mile back to his cabin. To complicate matters, he needed to do so without leaving a trail—no easy task in a foot of snow.

Today proved fun.

Tomorrow would be even more interesting, for he meant to kill whomever trespassed upon his land.

The next day, he packed only the essentials—ammunition, rations, water, a portable shelter, a pickaxe, and a shovel.

Moving carefully, quietly, he used the environment as camouflage. Other than the soft steps of his snowshoes, he remained soundless.

He intended to find the same spot as yesterday; to follow the tracks wherever they led. If necessary, his provisions would permit survival for days.

Almost an hour elapsed. When the sun broke through, he came across fresh boot prints. Prepared this time, he shouldered his rifle while dropping to his chest. He pointed the barrel toward the direction the tracks traveled.

As he peered through the scope, he saw the barrel of a rifle pointing back. That's all—just the barrel. He didn't see a man. He didn't even see an eye.

Just the barrel.

He scooted backward fifty yards before he got to his feet, turned, and ran.

It seemed he underestimated his opponent.

This would not occur again.

The deer meat sizzled in the pan when he heard the pounding against his door. Bears were known to paw at his cabin. He even once had an elk inexplicably ram it. He scared both of them off with a rifle blast. But this rapping utilized a cadence, a rhythm. Fortunately, he could employ the same tactic as against the animals. Gunfire frightened man even more than beast, for man understood the meaning of death and yearned to avoid it.

However, he had no doubt that the person outside his door would be the very same man who could have killed him. This threat wielded great intelligence and likely had a gun trained on the front door.

But who could it be? None took up residence this far out in the wilderness. No one had the stomach for the constant willpower, work, and pain it took to endure even a single day. He'd lived in that cabin for twenty-seven years; his survival was not by accident.

Whatever awaited him outside, it would *not* be the death of him.

The cabin featured no windows to reveal his movement. Throwing on a pair of boots and a parka, he next grabbed his rifle before sliding through a trap door that led out the back. With the temperature already below zero, he wouldn't last long wearing so little, but he didn't need much time for what he planned.

Ever so slightly, he crept along the cabin and then peeked around the corner with his rifle pointed at the front door.

He saw nobody in the waning light.

"Lower your weapon and face me."

He complied while turning, slowly, to see a well-insulated man standing behind him with a Colt .22 handgun held aloft. In his other hand, he clutched a case.

The stranger said, "What's your name?"

He refused to answer.

"All right, fine. Name's Cayden. I'm your neighbor."

He tightened his grip on the rifle, but left it pointing downward. Sting corrupted his fingers. Numbness would soon follow.

"Not the talking type, huh? Look, I know I'm not your neighbor in the traditional sense. After all, I had to travel over fifteen miles of public ground to get here. And, yeah, I admit I've been trespassing for a while now. Been watching you."

The rifle lifted a few inches.

"Look, I've been there for ten years. You didn't even know, did you?"

He couldn't suppress the shock upon his face.

"Yeah, you're good—a real survivalist. But me? I'm better. I've known about you for a decade and you didn't have a clue I existed until I left those prints for you."

The rifle almost reached a ninety-degree angle.

"I'll shoot you dead," Cayden warned. "I will. I'll shoot you dead, kick down your door, drag you in, and let the animals have at your carcass. If anyone ever finds this place, they'll think some bear had at you."

"What do you want?"

Cayden replied, "So you *can* talk. You're logical. Strategic. A good competitor."

His patience wore thin. If this would be to the death, he wanted it done already.

Cayden held up the case. He asked, "You want to play chess?"

"… You're serious."

Cayden answered. "Lately, I've felt a might lonely. Hoped we could have a standing game night."

"I don't play chess."

"I'll teach you," Cayden said.

"I didn't say I couldn't; I said I *don't*."

"If this takes any longer, you're going to freeze to death," Cayden said. "Either pull that trigger or invite me in. Your choice."

His fingers—he couldn't even feel them anymore.

"We'll have to go in the back way," he said. "Front door's barricaded."

While following him, Cayden asked, "You going to tell me your name?"

"No."

George Winthrop Jr. Park

"Look, there he is," Krystal groaned.

Ben said, "Every Tuesday! What's the creep doing at a children's park?"

Andrea added, "It'd be different if he brought a grandchild or something, but he just sits there watching the kids play in their bathing suits. It's weird!"

"We've done nothing about it this whole summer," Lisa said. "We should confront him. We need to let him know we're on to him. We can't tolerate it."

"Totally," Ben replied. "Doesn't he realize we see him gawking at our kids? He's lucky we haven't turned him over to the cops."

"So go tell him, Ben," Krystal prompted. "We shouldn't put this off any longer, and it'll sound more impressive coming from you."

"Why?" Ben asked. "Because I'm a man?"

"No," Krystal answered. "It's because you're super tall and probably three hundred pounds."

"Two-fifty," Ben huffed while getting to his feet. "Keep an eye on my Lacy, would you?"

Lisa smiled and said, "You bet, Ben. Good luck. We'll be here if things get out of hand."

Ben followed the water area's perimeter. Toddlers ran from spout to bucket to spray gun, laughing all the while. Ben had joined Lisa, Krystal, and Andrea's Tuesday play group after meeting them at church. Throughout the summer, they'd convened weekly at George Winthrop Jr. Park, and without fail, they'd seen the old man haunting a bench, speaking to no one, and ogling the children.

As Ben approached, he saw that the old man wore a battered fireman's cap and black-rimmed glasses, as well as a white shirt and blue jeans. He also had a thermos. Ben could only imagine its contents.

The man in question didn't notice Ben's advancement.

"Hey," Ben called out.

The man's head snapped away from the children and he studied Ben a moment, careful to avoid eye-contact. With a face devoid of friendliness, he mumbled, "Howdy."

No stranger to confrontation, Ben got right to the point by saying, "My friends and I notice that you come here a lot."

"Yep," the old man replied.

"Every Tuesday, in fact," Ben said.

"Just like you and yours," the man pointed out.

Ben chuckled a little before replying, "Yeah, but we bring our kids with us."

The old man went back to watching the children as he spat, "That right?"

Folding his arms across his wide chest, Ben answered, "Yeah, man. That's right."

Without looking at Ben, the man said, "I used to bring my kid to this park—every Tuesday. This was back before it had all the fancy water guns and such, back when it was still called Evergreen Park. It was a long time ago, probably before you were born."

"I don't really care," Ben replied. "I do care about my kid's safety, though, and I want to know what you're doi—"

"People are funny nowadays," the man interrupted. "They don't think. They don't think about the past or the future; they only think about the present. They get a notion, and they act on it, lickety-split."

"Look," Ben began, "I don't have time to listen to you rant, okay? I just wanted to give you fair warning: we don't like you watching our k—"

"You probably don't even know who George Winthrop Jr. is, do you?"

Furrowing his brow, Ben got caught off guard. He stammered, "W-What? No. Who cares about George Winthrop Jr.? He doesn't matter. It's just a park."

The old man laughed before grumbling, "He doesn't matter, huh? He sure mattered to Travis and Becky Swan. They had a little girl, about three years old, and she got trapped in her bedroom during a house fire. George Winthrop Jr. was a fireman, and he saved that little girl's life. He died doing it, but I'll be damned if he didn't get it done. The Swan girl got a little burned on her legs, but she went on to grow up and have a few kids of her own. Last I heard, she's teaching elementary school up north."

"Cool," Ben muttered, "so they changed the name of the park in honor of the fireman. I get it. What's your point?"

"Ha!" the old man cackled. "They changed it all right, but only after I hounded them for three solid years. A man gives his life saving a baby, and the city makes you jump through a thousand hoops just to give that man a little recognition. Then, a few more years go by, and before you know it, nobody even remembers who the park is named after."

Ben's cheeks grew hot as he began to understand.

The man continued, "Well, I'll always remember who this park is named after, I can tell you that much. My boy loved this park, and I know he'd love seeing all these kids enjoying it, too. Like I said, I brought him here every Tuesday, my only day off, and I don't aim to quit coming any time soon. Sometimes I can feel him sitting right on this bench next to me, and we watch the kids together, and we understand that he did right that night—saving that Swan girl. I miss him terrible, but he did the right thing, and I'm proud as hell of him."

Swallowing hard, Ben extended his hand and said, "I'm Ben Silvestri. Would you care to join my friends and me? You could meet our kids and maybe tell us a little bit more about your son."

The old man looked Ben in the eyes for the first time, and then, with his face brightening, said, "I'd like that."

Why We Won

I wore an inappropriate shade of pink, especially for the starting quarterback of a state championship game. Looking back, I guess it was a minor miracle that, at seventeen, I managed the laundry at all.

Truth be told, I really didn't care that night about my pink pants, and neither did anyone else on the team. We kept our minds focused on one thing—one thing only.

My mom had been sick for years … a lot of years. She did what she could for as long as she could, but her body eventually quit on her. When that happened, I took over. I cooked, cleaned the house, handled the odd jobs, and, obviously, did the laundry. The guys usually came over to help out. They knew my mom well by our senior year. Although she barely had any strength to speak, she used it to encourage them, to prop them up, to *love* them.

My dirtbag dad wasn't in the picture, but if you want to know how I felt about him, I imagined the back of his bald head every time I passed the football.

My station in life alarmed the other guys' parents. My intensity and its influence upon their sons scared them. But my squad … they knew what I was about. It didn't bother them if I didn't smile much or crack jokes. They understood that I played every game believing that if we won, my mom might win as well. They knew I believed it, and so they believed it, too. She wanted us to win; we wanted her to live. It proved a simple equation.

We started winning state championships in junior high, the same season my mom first got sick. She could still walk at that point. She marched right into practice, asked the coaches to leave, explained her diagnoses, and then demanded that we win as many games as we could before she died.

We didn't lose after that. Not a single game.

As a testament to my brothers' solidarity, the newspapers, the coaches, the teachers, the other parents, our opposition … they never got wind of it. If a guy left the team for whatever reason, he kept his mouth shut. They honored the pact made with my mother.

No one talked about *why* we won.

We just won.

And my mom lived.

But that night during our senior year, when I wore pink pants at the championship game, we didn't just win, we destroyed our competition. We broke their bones, we broke their will, and we broke their spirit to ever play the game again. We were later described as a pack of demons, monsters intent on crippling someone. They thought we played for Death himself, but it was actually the opposite.

My teammates knew I stayed up at night worrying about the ramifications of our final game. Naturally, our streak had to end. We talked about trying to make the same college team, but even the most optimistic of us grasped the impossibility of such a thing. During a private club meeting, we decided that if we played hard enough at the championship game, if we beat the other team badly enough, if we made *God* take notice of our victory, it might earn my mom a couple of extra years.

It didn't.

Thirty years have passed since she succumbed to cancer. Not a day goes by that I don't think of her. After high school, I tried walking onto my college's team, but I didn't really want to *play* at winning anymore. At least, not in regards to football. I wanted to win for real. Not at a game, but at life. My dad showed me how to quit. My mom taught me how to fight until the last breath.

Her life insurance paid for my schooling and then allowed me to open a business. I returned to my hometown, married a teacher new to the area, and started a family. Though I resembled my dad, that's all I had in common with the bastard. I *liked* being a family man.

Most of the guys came back for our thirtieth reunion. After the official ceremony at the high school, I invited them to my restaurant. They all made good in their own way. Every single one of them could count themselves a success.

We got to talking and each revealed the secret of their achievements. They said it was my mom and me. Watching me fight for my mom, watching my mom fight for life, it gave them perspective. Whenever they faced an obstacle, they tackled it with my mom's tenacity.

I couldn't believe it. These men, my brothers, cared about my mother—about *me*—so deeply, that even after thirty years, long after leaving the turf behind, they still fought and won on our behalf.

After the reunion, I decided to volunteer with the local football team. They've lost for far too long. I'm going to tell them about my mom. I'm going to ask them what's going on in their lives that they *need* to beat.

I'm going to help them find a reason to win.

Cold Turkey

Eddie stands fuming outside in the bitter cold while his son, wife, and in-laws sit at the dinner table surrounding a cold turkey.

How did such woeful events occur on Thanksgiving Day? Read on …

As his favorite football team seemed determined to get trounced on national television, Eddie decided he saw enough. He rose from his father-in-law's recliner, made his way to the front hall, retrieved his coat, then backtracked across the living room and traveled through the kitchen while enjoying its delicious aromas. His six-year-old son colored at the little-used kitchen table and they exchanged wordless smiles before Eddie reached the back door.

As soon as Eddie stepped into the frigid November air, he reached into his left coat pocket.

Nothing.

He tried the right pocket.

Equally barren.

Charging back into the house, Eddie once again noticed the smell of cooking turkey while he rumbled past his son and through the kitchen.

He found his wife and in-laws waiting for him in the living room with the television turned off. They wore expressions of trepidation.

"Susan," Eddie said to his wife of eleven years, "where are my cigarettes?"

"Eddie," she began after a quick glance to her parents, "you've been promising us for years. We talked it over, and we decided to take matters into our own hands."

"You mean you stole my cigarettes?" Eddie asked in disbelief. "You took them right out of my coat pocket?"

Her eyes pleading, Susan said, "We knew you didn't have a secret stash here; we figured this was our best chance to prove you don't need them. If you can get through today, then you can get through the rest of the week, and then the month, and then maybe even the year …"

Eddie, bewildered, looked at his in-laws and questioned, "Donna, Marvin—you two were part of this?"

"We love you like our own flesh and blood, Eddie," Marvin said with his palms up. "I know it was a dirty thing to do, but we did it because we care so much about you."

Donna amended, "We want you around for a long time so you can raise that boy of ours. My father died from emphysema. He smoked his entire life, just like you're doing. Do you want your son to go fatherless?"

Detecting her husband's rage, Susan confessed, "This seemed like our best option—our only option."

His eyes narrowed to slits. Eddie said nothing in response to his family. Instead, he spun on his heel and plowed through the house once more. Of course, to make his way to the back door, he had to enter the kitchen anew, and when he did so, the smell of succulent turkey filled his nostrils again and made his mouth water.

A petty, underhanded idea invaded Eddie's mind.

He stopped right in front of the oven. He turned his head ever so slightly and saw his son still engrossed with his coloring book, paying Eddie no attention at all. In one deft movement, Eddie did the unthinkable.

It would be hours before anyone noticed.

Now that you know why Eddie endures the freezing elements and his family sits staring at a half-cooked turkey, we shall conclude our misadventure. Can any good possibly come of such calamity? We shall see …

"Daddy?" Eddie's son asks as he pokes his head out the door.

"Yeah?" Eddie replies. His face is flushed and his voice quivers both from anger and the icy temperature. But when he looks into his son's eyes, his fury subsides. He thinks of the mess he's made of their Thanksgiving.

"Daddy, aren't you going to come sit with us? We're all waiting for you at the table."

Eddie figures Susan, Donna, and Marvin didn't disclose his transgression to the boy.

"Um, I don't really think the turkey's fit to eat this year," Eddie says.

"Yeah, but aren't we still supposed to join hands and give thanks?" his son asks. "Isn't that what today's all about? I mean, that's what we've been doing since I was a little kid."

Before taking a deep breath, Eddie recognizes that he's the biggest turkey of all.

"You're right—you're exactly right. Let's go in and I'll first give thanks for having the world's wisest six-year-old, then I'll apologize to your mom and grandparents and give thanks for their love and—hopefully—forgiveness."

Eddie sees his son looking at him knowingly.

"You saw me do it, didn't you?" Eddie asks.

Nodding, the boy returns, "I didn't tell. I think they figured it out, though. Don't worry, you and Mommy always tell me if you say you're sorry, people will forgive you."

With moist eyes, Eddie takes his son's outstretched hand and says, "I'm sorry to you, too. Do you forgive me?"

"I forgive you, Daddy," his son replies. Then, looking up at his father with a bright, semi-toothless smile, he asks, "Can we order a pizza?"

Eddie laughs as they reenter the house and says, "Yep, and I believe I'll be buying. Just don't get used to pizza on Thanksgiving. This is our last year of cold turkey."

Depths

"Mr. Ben?"

"Yeah, Raph?"

"I prefer my full name, Mr. Ben."

"My apologies, *Raphael*. What's up?"

Children surrounded a plastic banquet table as they toiled away at a craft pertaining to Jonah and the whale. The Youth Ministry Team created an engineering marvel in which the Sunday school students could color a previously manufactured Jonah, affix him to a craft stick, and then connect that to the back of a large cardboard whale. With the help of a grommet, the children could force the whale to regurgitate Jonah and then swallow him whole again.

Luckily for everyone, Ben wasn't in charge of developing such projects. He simply facilitated class every Sunday morning in room 21 of the church basement.

Encouraged by Ben, Raphael asked, "Do fish utilize a digestive system comparable to that of a human?"

Baylee, Ben's daughter, said, "See? I told you Raphael was smart, Dad."

Another child, Kean, countered: "I'm just as smart." Though he listened intently, Kean refused to divert his eyes from the shade of gray he hoped to achieve by alternating between the heavy application of a black crayon and the soft smattering of a white.

"Guys, it's not a competition," Ben said.

"That's good," Jay giggled, "because I'd lose big time!"

Baylee, Hattie, Malik, and Sammy joined Jay in laughter. Kean didn't appear to find it all that funny while Raphael seemed not to notice the joke at all.

"Mr. Ben?" Raphael repeated.

"Right, Raph—*Raphael*—sorry. Fish. Um, yeah. I think fish digest food the same way we do ..."

"I can check on my phone," Baylee offered.

Kean muttered, "Cell phones are not allowed in Sunday school classes."

"We can't get a signal down here anyway," Sammy added. "It's like a dungeon."

"Mr. Ben?" Raphael asked.

"Yes, Raphael," Ben responded as he strolled along the perimeter of the room.

Raphael said, "Jonah could not survive in the stomach of a whale. He would have been digested by the third day."

"Oh," Ben began, "well, you see, the Bible is … um, we shouldn't take everything the Bible says literally, right?"

"What?" Hattie huffed. "My mom says the Bible is *truth*."

Nodding furiously, Ben replied, "Yes! It is. It is truth—that's right."

Sammy said, "But … you just said it shouldn't be taken literally."

"What does 'literally' mean again?" Jay asked.

Malik answered, "You know, like, *word for word*."

Kean mumbled, "You were right about being the loser in the room …"

"Kean," Ben said, "come on, that's not nice."

"You were saying, Mr. Ben," Raphael prompted.

Perspiration seeped from Ben's forehead. "Oh. Well, that was pretty much it. It's just that, while—yes—the Bible is truth, most people agree that it also uses quite a bit of embellishment in order to make a point."

Raphael asked, "So it's possible Jonah did not actually find himself swallowed by a whale, fish, or any other aquatic lifeform?"

Hattie's eyes bored through Ben as he said, "… It's possible."

Malik leaned over to Sammy and whispered, "Mr. Ben is so fired."

Having overheard the comment, Baylee declared, "My dad does this for free. He can't be fired."

"He could be asked to step down," Kean said.

Ben and his wife joined Mt. Calvary Evangelical Lutheran Church twelve years ago when they were engaged. They were young, new to the community, and felt an urge to assimilate. Though they were now longstanding members of the church, they still knew very few people. Ben thought that teaching his daughter's Sunday school class could be a productive way to increase his connectivity to the congregation.

Forcing himself to laugh, Ben said, "I don't think anyone is going to ask me to step down."

"You look apprehensive, Mr. Ben," Raphael said.

Ben asked, "Are you sure you're only eight? You're all eight, right?"

"Yes, Dad, we're all eight, about to turn nine."

"I'm already nine," Malik said.

Hattie added, "Me, too."

"Mr. Ben, may I ask you a difficult question?"

Sensing Raphael's trajectory, Ben wanted to preemptively deny the child's request. Unfortunately, he didn't wield the ability to redirect or otherwise terminate Raphael's impending inquiry.

Mistaking Ben's silence as accordance, Raphael pressed on by asking, "Do you believe in God?"

"Duh!" Jay exclaimed. "He wouldn't be teaching Sunday school if he didn't."

Ben moved his mouth, but nothing came out.

"I only ask," Raphael continued, "because I find it very confusing. So much of the Bible is impossible. There is no evidence of God's existence in modern day society. Yet, in Biblical times, God's influence manifested regularly. I hoped you could provide some insight."

The children grew quiet. Each one of them, even Kean, awaited Ben's reply.

Ben thought for a moment, then said, "You're all so smart. So much smarter than I was at your age. I'll just be honest with you. I struggle with God all the time. I don't teach Sunday school due to a calling or anything like that. I just wanted to spend more time with Baylee, help out the church, get to know some kids, and maybe meet your parents."

The children remained silent.

"So do I believe in God?" Ben resumed. "… Yes, I do, but I don't really know *why*. Maybe it's because my parents raised me in the church? Maybe I've been conditioned to believe? I don't know. And I won't lie to you—I can't say that I believe everything in the Bible to be true. A lot of it doesn't make any sense at all. I guess it just comes down to … faith."

Ben watched the children nod in agreement. Only Hattie seemed dissatisfied with Ben's analysis.

As they returned to their crafts, Raphael said, "Thank you, Mr. Ben. I appreciate your candor."

"Um, you're welcome."

Raphael worked on his project for a few more moments, then looked up and asked, "Could we discuss Santa Claus?"

At that point, Jay erupted, "Dude! Don't even go there!"

The Easter Egg Escapade

So there he is, my only son, about to be pummeled by a throng of angry parents.

I can't say I blame them. Way back when he was a little guy, if some strange man stole Easter eggs right from kids' baskets the way my boy is, why, I'd be obliged to serve up a knuckle sandwich as well.

His pretty little girlfriend—and she is still *just* his girlfriend, by the by—is pleading with the hapless fool to leave the poor children alone. Of course, she doesn't have a clue why he's seemingly gone off the deep end and decided to terrorize children barely old enough to remember their own addresses.

I get it, though. I understand his motivations exactly. When he piled us in the car this morning and said we were heading out to Old Bruns' Field, I'd already figured out what he had in mind. I considered it a bad idea at the time, and his current state only reaffirms my original notion.

Anyway, I better get involved soon. After all, this has the potential to be great for business. Besides, like I said, he's my only son. Be a shame to lose him over Easter eggs.

In the meantime, let me catch you up.

Last night, Abe—that's my boy; you know, the one about to do his impression of an eggplant—disappeared. He said he had a top-secret mission. As a teenager, such erratic behavior wouldn't have surprised us much. But seeing as how he's now in his late twenties and brought his girlfriend to our place for Easter weekend, well, we considered it fairly odd.

Teri—that's his girlfriend—was polite enough about it. They'd been together for several years, and she had gotten to know us pretty well. So while he was off doing whatever, we sat around the kitchen table, played Scrabble, and joked about Abe's display of absurdity.

When Abe finally returned home with dust all over his shoes and a face beaten red by the cold night air, it didn't take much for my old brain to add two and two. Luckily for him, neither my wife, Cara, nor Teri guessed what Abe had been up to.

Teri even went so far as to tease Abe about having a woman on the side.

I believe that could be considered irony.

The idea of dragging him back out into the dark and revealing the faultiness of his plan crossed my mind, but I didn't want to alert Teri and ruin anything. I just figured I'd have to bail him out the next day. Before Cara and I went to bed, I grabbed a stack of free passes out of my work desk and put them next to my wallet on the nightstand. They'd come in handy later.

So Easter morning, after Abe cajoled us out of bed and into his car, he drove us to Old Bruns' Field. I could tell by his panic at the sight of dozens of parked vehicles along the road that he'd neglected to remember the town's churches came together annually and held an Easter egg hunt for the little ones a few hours before services started. How my boy could have forgotten such a fact is beyond me. His mother and I only brought him to this very field for this very event every Easter until he was ten.

When boys are in love, they seem to turn noodle-brained.

Abe's not really one to lose his cool, so while I'd foreseen his predicament, I hadn't counted on him going nuttier than a fruitcake and snatching kids' Easter eggs straight from their baskets. He'd take a plastic egg, pop it open, then toss it to the ground when he saw candy or a toy escape. The poor kid he'd plundered would then scoop up the bounty with tear-stained cheeks while Abe picked out a new victim.

Teri ran after him as he raced from child to child, pleading with him to stop. Before long, quite a few young mothers and fathers confronted my son with some pretty hefty threats. Had it not been a church crowd, Abe may not have been given that courtesy. They might have just knocked him down and been done with it.

And that's where we are.

I tell everyone to calm down, and, because of my gray hair and the fact they're a respectful lot, they listen. Abe looks to be near hyperventilation when I ask the little ones if they want to see that latest Disney movie, the one that just happens to be playing at my dollar theater. Of course, I see a horde of tiny hands shoot into the air. I reach into my coat pocket and pull out the stack of passes I'd brought along— each good for one free viewing. I explain to them that in order to get a free pass, all they have to do is form a line in front of the deranged lunatic—my son—and let him peek into their eggs.

It's probably no surprise the little rascals fall into formation faster than I can say "Jiminy Cricket."

Abe investigates a good forty eggs with trembling hands and a sweaty brow before I start to doubt whether the particular egg in question had yet to be found.

But at last, he cries out in joy.

I smile as I watch him return the artificial egg to the little girl without its prize—a diamond ring.

As Abe drops to one knee and takes Teri by the hand, the adults in the crowd finally understand what had him so riled up and they start to cheer. And Teri, why, she must be as crazy as my boy, because she says "yes" without delay.

For my part, well, I'm just glad to pick up a little extra business. Kids get in free—sure.

But I didn't say anything about their parents.

Drive By

I stand by the window, looking out, watching my daughter play in the front yard.

My heart fills with dread.

They should be here any minute.

Should being the operative word.

Will they come?

Why should they?

I'm amazed how everyone seems to know everyone—everyone but me. How do they all know each other? Our kids are in third grade. When I was a kid, if my classmates didn't live in the neighborhood, my parents didn't know their parents at all.

I seem to be the only one upholding that tradition. How would I even begin to meet the other kids' parents? PTO? Sports?

I honestly have no idea.

I don't want my daughter to pay for my ignorance. She's going to be the outcast. The weirdo. The kid with the dad who's clueless about throwing birthday parties under ordinary circumstances. But during a pandemic? Hopeless.

When the mom emailed, my instinct said not to trust her.

She wanted to organize a birthday parade for my daughter. She said my daughter's teacher asked her to do it, which is also how she got my email address. She said she'd be happy to lend a hand—I just needed to make sure my daughter hung out in the front yard at a certain time. She included her phone number and asked me to call.

I did.

It wasn't bad, but it was awful.

Against my better judgement, I agreed to it. I asked if I could assist, and—to my relief—she said not to worry about a thing.

Why?

She doesn't know me. I'm not even sure she knows my daughter. She owes me nothing—no favors, no kindness, no mercy. Yet, she supposedly got in touch with all the kids' families and set up a parade.

But what if she didn't? What if she changed her mind? What if she got busy with her actual friends or her real commitments?

I'm expected to trust her without knowing her.

Maybe I should have just thrown a party. Screw it. Get the bouncy house. Hire the clown. Order pizza. Invite the entire third grade to our backyard. Pandemic be damned.

No.

I couldn't bring myself to do that. It would have been hard when things were normal—but I would have done it. I keep telling myself I would have bitten the bullet and hosted a party.

But now? I can't bring myself to take that risk. No matter how unlikely, I can't jeopardize my daughter's health.

The neighborhood thinks I'm a freak for taking this so seriously. My daughter will likely be ostracized for the rest of her school years because of me. She'll be the kid with the nutty dad. The house nobody wants to come visit. She won't be invited places because no one will want to deal with me.

What they must think—all those normal parents. I can't even organize a birthday parade on my own.

What's *wrong* with me?

I watch my daughter.

She's the only bright spot in my life. The only thing I got right. I'm doing the best I can, but I'm not equipped for parenthood. It doesn't come naturally. I never expected to be doing it alone.

I watch her.

My heart is full of joy, fear, confusion, love, anxiety, and happiness all at once.

Tears zigzag down my face.

For the longest time, nothing happens but the hitch of my chest.

And then I hear it—a blaring of horns. I see my daughter begin to jump up and down, waving her arms. Cars and minivans appear. Most have balloons attached. Some even have her name written on the sides, wishing her a happy birthday.

She looks at me through the window, gestures for me to come outside, and then goes back to jumping for joy.

I wipe off the tears, walk to the front door, and reach for the knob.

The Back Pew

Alice Goddard attended St. John's Lutheran her entire life. She was baptized in the eloquent old church twenty-nine years ago by Pastor Stone, who had long since left and later died, rest his soul. She went to Sunday school without falter, took part in Catechism, and was confirmed in the eighth grade—there she publicly vowed her allegiance to Jesus Christ. She later married a man named Richard, whom everyone called 'Dick,' when she was twenty-one. They reared two children, Clive and Anthony, during their four years of marriage, and then they divorced. Somehow, Richard got custody of the children. He then moved to Madison, Wisconsin, in pursuit of a high school sweetheart.

Alice gave up believing in God around the time the state granted Dick her children, but, as was her custom, she never missed a church service.

There was a time when her friends would have come to her rescue and taken her mind off so many problems, but they all left town for various reasons or became so busy with their own children that they didn't have enough time to use the bathroom, let alone tend to her desperate needs.

The current pastors—Hadden, Byus, and Scholfield—each visited her empty home on several occasions, quoting Scripture and inviting her to church functions, but Alice always presented some reason or another as to why she couldn't visit such things. She did, however, sit and listen quietly as they reiterated the Gospel and reminded her of the wonderful Christian she had once been. They vowed to her that God was waiting for her to come back to Him, she just had to open her heart again.

But by that point, it was too late. She had already decided that if God was going to turn His back on her, she would do the same.

However, a lifetime of being in a certain room at a certain time could not be broken, so she continued to attend St. John's, sitting silently in the back pew—alone.

One Sunday, near the end of January, a young man sat in front of her, breaking the boundary the congregation unconsciously established around Alice Goddard. He was apparently a visitor to the church, for Alice had never seen him before. He wore a dark brown sports coat, the kind you could get for under thirty dollars, a pair of jeans, and a plain white shirt. His hair was a deep oatmeal, unkempt, and somewhat greasy.

Pastor Byus began the morning announcements, and then initiated the opening hymn. Alice was certain she could hear the man singing, but it wasn't nearly loud enough to appoint as a falsetto or baritone. In fact, he seemed to be one of those people who sang just above a whisper.

She once had a beautiful voice, but she quit making a sound of any sort while at church, and, frankly, outside of it as well.

Then came the dreaded moment when all were supposed say, "Peace be with you," to whomever sat nearby. Fortunately for Alice, as already established, no one ever sat near enough for it to be an issue. None came to her, nor did she make any attempt to go to them.

"Now take a moment to greet those around you," Pastor Byus prompted.

Alice lowered her eyes and hoped the man would be shy—shy or rude. Either one was fine with her.

No such luck.

He turned to face her with his brown eyes catching the winter sunlight through the windows. She lifted her eyes and noticed his light beard.

"Peace be with you?" he asked while extending his hand. They were ragged and calloused.

He raised an interested eyebrow when she said nothing in return, but instead, literally turned her entire body so that her back was to him. He clenched his outstretched hand into a confused, passive fist, flattened out his modest sports coat, then turned to the people in front of him.

Alice slowly spun back around when the service resumed. She was shocked when the man remained seated at the end of the service.

Again, he turned around gradually, cautiously, and faced her once more. She lifted her eyes until they met his own, but she said nothing—not an apology, not an excuse, nothing.

"Are you okay?" he asked.

She nodded once.

"Do you need to talk?"

She shook her head.

"You sure?"

Before Alice could answer, some congregation members stood at the end of the man's pew, welcoming him to their church. He smiled politely to Alice, then walked down the length of the pew to converse with them.

Her eyes followed the visitor as he approached those who forsook her. They held a nice conversation with him, laughing and smiling, doing all the things that humans are supposed to do when they take joy in being a Christian and living a Christian life. She'd been one of them once, before everything she loved about her life was ripped away.

The next week, like clockwork, she sat silently in the last pew at the ten-fifteen traditional service. It was Communion Sunday, and this would mark the fifty-fifth consecutive Communion she chose not to receive.

After about four missed Communions, some friends in the congregation attempted to persuade her to reintroduce Christ into her system again, both spiritually and physically. She instead chose to insult their idealistic, utopian lives and sent them away. Those friends never contacted her again. Alice decided they were total failures as Christians. She didn't consider herself a disappointment, though. Her disdain for God and Christ was a conscious decision, not some accidental shortcoming due to lack of character.

At any rate, for the second straight Sunday, there was the mysterious man. Wearing the same outfit, he sat down, looked over his shoulder, and nodded at Alice with a sincere but wary smile. She looked away from his kindness, finding it both pretentious and awkward.

There they were, one in front of the other, without any sort of communication at all until the greetings. Once more, he faced her, held out his chapped hands, and said, "Peace be with you."

This time he uttered it as though an order. His voice was solid, and because of his sureness, she couldn't help but reach for him. She took his hand and found that it was indeed quite coarse. As they shook, she glanced about the church and saw that the entire congregation gawked at them.

Her hand shot out of his.

"I'm Josh."

"Alice," she mumbled.

"Nice to meet you, Alice."

Josh was then pulled away by the people in front of him who did not realize what a pivotal moment this was in Alice's life, for she was about to return the sentiment, making more progress than she had in years. Josh had no choice but to turn and greet those before him in order to grant them peace as well. He would not turn anyone away.

When it came time to rise and take Communion, Alice despised herself when she realized she would take it if only Josh invited her to walk with him.

But Josh did not invite her, because he did not rise himself.

At the end of the service, Josh stood, stared at Alice for just a moment with a pleasant look upon his face, and said, "It's nice to see you again."

"You, too," she muttered. She forgot how to talk civilly with someone. However, she told the truth. It *was* nice to see him again.

"Why do you sit back here?" he asked.

Although it strained her to maintain the conversation, she pressed on: "I don't believe in God anymore."

He said, "Not really sure what you're doing here, then."

She didn't respond, so he continued by saying, "Yeah, it can be hard, can't it? I mean, He used to talk to people directly all the time, like it was going on every other day, whereas now, well, not many of us have that sort of familiarity with Him. And His son, wow, that's a hard one to swallow, too, huh?"

"What do you mean?" she asked, her eyes becoming alert.

"Well, they want us to believe that two thousand years ago some guy who was supposed to be God in human form died for our sins? Where's the proof? I mean, the Bible? That's the proof? That's not much for today's Information Age, is it? Seeing is believing, and no one's seen Jesus in quite some time."

Beyond belief, Alice found herself growing argumentative, countering with, "Maybe we see Him more often than we think. Maybe He just doesn't walk up to us and say, 'Hey, I'm Jesus, what's up?'"

"Oh, come on, Alice," Josh laughed, "you don't really think Jesus walks among us ..."

Before she met Richard, the man many called Dick, she fervently believed such a thing possible—that it was even a fact. Finally, she whispered, "I think He could, maybe He doesn't, but I think He could."

Josh walked around his edge of the wooden pew, then sat down next to her. "Alice, you either think He does or He doesn't, you can't take a 'maybe' position on this."

Meeting his brown eyes with her own green ones, Alice thought a moment, bit down on her lip, then confessed, "When I was younger, even as a little girl, I swore I saw Jesus sitting here, right where you are now."

"That's ridiculous," Josh chuckled.

"It's not ridiculous," she disagreed. "He sat back here all the time. Even at my wedding, I told the ushers not to seat anyone in that spot. Guess what? He walked in just as the ceremony started."

"Really? What did He wear?" Josh asked.

"Kind of what you're wearing," Alice replied.

"Seriously?"

"Of course," Alice replied. "He always wore nice clothes, I mean, nice enough. Just nice enough to show respect in His Father's house, but never

showy, never too glamorous. You've got his style,"
she said while narrowing her eyes.

"I dress like this because I'm poor," Josh
answered with a grin, "not because I choose to."

"What do you do for a living?" she asked.

"Carpenter."

She felt a wave of euphoria wash over her
heart, something she used to believe was the Holy
Spirit, and she cried.

"Why are you crying?" Josh asked, reaching
out and taking her hand as he did so.

She did not pull away.

"I've been telling myself and everyone who
would listen to me that I reject God," she sobbed. "I'm
not mad at God. I'm mad a Richard!"

"Don't most people call him 'Dick?'"

With laughter and tears, Alice confirmed,
"Rightly so."

"I want you to make me a promise," Josh
demanded while squeezing her hand.

"What?" she asked, paying no heed to the
tears rolling down her cheeks.

"I want you to sit with your pastors and talk
things out. Real talk, no holding back due to pride or

resentment. Tell them the truth, even if you think you shouldn't. Trust me, pastors have made mistakes in their pasts—that's just part of being human, right? That's why He died for us, right?"

"Yeah," Alice choked.

"Good. It's okay to be mad at God, Alice. Everyone gets mad at God at some point in their lives. But you can't stay mad at Him, not if you truly believe. He's given far more than He will ever take."

"He took my sons," Alice cried.

"No, Dick took your sons, and that's because the judge owed him a favor. You were supposed to appeal his decision, remember? But you didn't; you lost heart, stopped praying, turned your back on the church and God, and descended into this shadow of your former self. You came to rely on Dick more than your creator, and when Dick left, you revoked your entire foundation. But God is always willing to take you back, no matter how long you've been away. He's been waiting."

"Yes," Alice responded.

Josh stood up, flattened out his sports jacket, nodded at the pastors who watched incredulously along with some of the congregation, and called out,

"Hey, do you think you could whip up a Communion for her? It's been a while."

The pastors all but fell over themselves as they rushed to the front of the church, and the ushers sprinted as fast as their legs would allow for the materials they needed.

"Will you take it with me?" Alice asked as she held onto his rough hands.

"Me?" he asked with a grin. "Oh, I don't think so."

"Of course," Alice said while closing her eyes.

Josh let go of Alice's hand, then said, "You keep your promise, because God will keep His. Okay?"

"We're ready," Pastors Hadden and Schofield said as they stood with joy in their hearts at the front of St. John's Lutheran Church.

There would be many apologies in the coming weeks, both from Alice and to her as well. For all were in the wrong, and it took only the reminder of their purpose to bring them together again.

"I'll keep my promise," Alice pledged before opening her eyes.

"Say 'hi' to the kids for me, and even Richard, too," Josh said before he started to walk away.

As she approached the alter, Alice reminded, "Most people call him 'Dick.'"

"Rightly so," Josh said with the flash of a smile before moving along.

A Man Out Of Time

Jenna sat next to her grandfather at the Academy Awards in a dress designed by someone whose name proved too sesquipedalian to pronounce. Mateo, of course, wore nothing but the best, though he wore it in hues long outdated and cuts antiquated.

Mateo Sandoval found himself nominated for the eleventh time. He first earned a nomination in 1946 for playing a tormented Confederate Civil War medic trapped by an abolitionist woman who kept him chained to her woodstove, vowing he would not be released until the war ended. Mateo acted superbly in the film, but he did not win that year—the award went to Frederic March. Nor two years later when Olivier took it. Nor seven years after that when they gave it to William Holden. The decades passed with him nominated time after time, but he never triumphed.

This year his nomination arrived by playing an atheist who, after living to see his wife, children, and grandchildren all die under tragic circumstances, took Christ into his heart only so that when he died and went to Heaven, he could personally kill God. The role proved demanding, but he pulled it off magnificently. Many felt this year would be his.

Jenna always prioritized her grandfather's best interests. Her job that night wasn't much different than their daily lives together. Because Mateo refused to wear hearing aids, she often clarified things for him. After much discussion, they decided when he won for Best Actor, she simply had to lean in and let him know as such. Though they spoke of him perhaps losing, neither could accept that possibility.

Thus, when Julian Howard's name reverberated through the speakers, none appeared more shocked than Jenna as she threw her hands up and thrust back into her seat. She bumped Mateo, which prompted him to arise. He mirrored the winner's movement as they both approached the stage from opposite ends.

Mr. Howard, a man of thirty-three, wore a perplexed expression upon his face as Mateo took the statue from the presenter and stood directly before the microphone. The applause quickly died down, and it appeared as though Mateo believed it did so out of reverence. Jenna suspected it rather the result of universal embarrassment.

However, her own heart swelled, for at long last her grandfather held the award he deserved.

Mr. Howard, sensing the awkwardness, simply took his place alongside the presenters and watched as his idol accepted an Oscar that, while not awarded, certainly had been earned.

"I'd like to thank the Academy," Mateo said, "for finally coming to its senses." He laughed and did not look troubled when no one else joined. "You have no idea how much I've always wanted to say that."

The orchestra music played, softly yet inauspiciously, and Mateo bellowed, "I've waited over five decades for this award; there is no way in holy Hell you're going to play this best actor off stage!"

He next shook the Oscar high over his head and beamed from ear to ear. The crowd could not help but put their hands together in support of the sheer vitality displayed by their favorite luminary.

The orchestra music wisely placated.

"Thank you," Mateo offered with an open-handed gesture to the conductor. "As I was saying, I've been in this game for many, many years. I've worked with the best and the worst. I've lived a good life, and now I can die happily. I know that sounds silly to some of you, but when an artist pours his heart—his very soul—into his work and that effort is never commended by the greatest awards show in the world … well, that can prove burdensome.

"Some would give up. Hell, I've known a lot that did. Not me, though. I knew one way or the other, by God, I was going to get up on this stage, even if in the twilight of my career—my very life—and finally hold this award. And look, here I am."

A roar of applause erupted, led by Jenna.

"I've got to be honest with you, this film wasn't my favorite. The director's an egomaniacal prick; my costars rigid and unnatural; and frankly, I thought the script self-serving and pompous. However, I knew it had the stuff of controversy, Oscar's favorite skirt, so I plunged in headfirst like any horny boy would!"

Here he chuckled a little. A few accompanied him, but most were losing faith again.

"Despite its utter tastelessness, I knew Hollywood would lap it up with the usual fervor it displays for gourmet shit, and so I made a point to give it my all. You could say that for me, it was Oscar or bust.

"Well, thank God … it's not bust," Mateo sighed. "It's Oscar. Finally, it's Oscar."

Mateo's eyes glistened and he paused while holding his fist up to his mouth. He looked away from his audience for the briefest of moments, and then, with a renewed flourish of intensity, said, "I want to thank you all for watching my movies. Chasing this castrated little boy is what's kept me alive these last few decades. Hell, the Academy did me a favor. They added years to my life!"

Jenna noted that some of the crowed laughed and nearly all smiled. He had his Oscar, just as everyone wanted, and so the world turned a little more gracefully.

"If I die tomorrow, or the day after that," Mateo said with the award clutched to his chest, "don't mourn for me. I am satisfied."

This time, when the music floated up, he said, "Now I truly *am* a man out of time. Thank you—thank you for this moment."

He grinned at Jenna. She winked in return with a mischievous smile.

The crowed rose and offered a standing ovation, Mateo's last.

A Christmas Confrontation

James Henderson shook the snow from his overcoat and dress shoes as he entered the mammoth church. In his opinion—with the food court, café, gift shop, and free Wi-Fi—it had more in common with a shopping mall. His left hand clung to a hot pink flier so tightly that his knuckles turned stark white.

James pounded through the lobby, but the grey carpet devoured his stomps, rendering them ineffectual. Teenagers loitered around everywhere. Some were working on homework, but most were playing on their phones or gossiping. Nearly all of them clutched a coffee of some sort. They obviously came straight over once school dismissed. This fact only served to enrage James all the more.

He stopped one of them, a boy whose hair hid his eyes, and demanded to know the location of the youth minister's office. After a muffled response, James headed in the appropriate direction. He hadn't bothered to wipe his feet, and so he left cold, wet tracks behind him.

The particular door he sought stood wide open. James burst into the office without knocking or announcing himself in any way. He discovered an older man sitting at a desk, listening to a radio show while tapping away on his laptop. The man wore a white Chicago Bears hat, a red pullover, and a silver wedding ring. The office was adorned with posters promoting musical groups unfamiliar to James— names like Switchfoot, Third Day, and David Crowder Band.

Before the older man could even look up, James huffed, "My name's James Henderson, and I expect a word with Marty Yaple."

The other man didn't seem startled by the rash intrusion whatsoever, as though unexpected outbursts were an everyday occurrence in his world. He smiled and said, "You're looking at him."

"No," James said. "I want to see Marty Yaple, the youth minister."

"Yeah, that's still me. I'm Marty."

James squinted at the man, prompting Marty to say, "Ministering to youth doesn't mean the minister has to be young in body, though being young in spirit helps. I really am Marty Yaple. Now, what can I do for you?"

As James rushed across the room and slammed the pink flier down upon Marty's desk, the youth minster pushed a button on his laptop. This brought the radio show to an end.

"You're responsible for this," James seethed.

Marty looked at the flier, then said, "I take it you don't like the event."

"No, Mr. Yaple—"

"Call me Marty—"

"Mr. Yaple, I do not like the event one bit. *Get Jiggy With Jesus' Birthday.* It's sacrilegious."

Having had many experiences over the years with people of all temperaments, Marty remembered to keep his cool. "We're celebrating the birth of Christ on Christmas Eve. *Jiggy* denotes joy, dancing, and celebration. Where's the blasphemy in that?"

Scooping the flier back up, James read, "Live music, dancing, pizza, video games." With his nostrils flaring and a vein above his left brow visibly throbbing, he interrogated, "Where's Communion? Candles? Hymns? What about a sermon? You don't mention anything that remotely gives the impression of worship."

Marty felt his cheeks flush ever so slightly as he said, "Well, to be fair, Mr. Henderson, we're celebrating Jesus' birth. We will pray as a group, of course, and I always encourage independent prayer as well, but we want it to be a party. We'll address those things you mentioned the next day during regular service, but our youth Christmas Eve event is all about celebrating Jesus' arrival into the world and our hearts by throwing a party."

Skepticism shrouded James' face. Marty witnessed that look a thousand times during his years of service. Waving the flier back and forth as though aflame, James growled, "My thirteen-year-old daughter brought this home yesterday from school. One of her friends, a member of your youth group, gave it to her. She wants to come."

"Wonderful!" Marty exclaimed.

"Wrong, Mr. Yaple. My wife and I have taken her to our church's Christmas Eve service since she was a little girl. Now that tradition will come to an end over pizza and live music? Our family will spend its first Christmas Eve apart over some gimmick? How can you justify the turmoil you're bringing into my family by catering to the whims of children?"

Though a Godly man, Marty felt anger swell up inside his chest. He didn't deny it; instead, he overcame it. He said, "My goal as youth minister is to bring children to Christ so that they may then bring their future children to Christ. You may not like my methodology, but I firmly believe Christmas is about Jesus; we want to celebrate Him."

Marty noticed that James' expression slightly softened as he continued with, "Look, Mr. Henderson, we're both Christians. We may not have the same ideologies, but we both believe in Christ and want your daughter to celebrate Him. Now, we'd love to have her join us, but as long as she's acknowledging His birth, I'm a happy man wherever she is."

And then Marty spotted it.

Up until that point, he believed he saw anger in James' eyes. But he was mistaken. It was not anger James suffered, but pain. Marty, being the father of three grown women, finally realized what was at the heart of this confrontation.

Marty asked, "You said your daughter is thirteen?"

James simply nodded with averted eyes placed upon a nearby cross.

"I remember those days. That's around the time they realize we're not infallible; that maybe our way isn't always the best. And then something like this comes along, and you ask yourself, 'Man, if she's willing to break a Christmas tradition of all things, what's next?' And that thought scares the hell out of you, just like it did me."

When James looked at Marty once more, the old youth minister saw tears.

"She's going to grow up, James, and she's going to live a life without you there by her side. Trust me, there's not a thing you can do to stop it, nor should you. But just remember Proverbs: 'Train up a child in the way he should go: and when he is old, he will not depart from it.'"

"That's from the King James version of the Bible," James said.

"It is," Marty replied.

"I assumed you to be an NIV man."

Marty grinned and said, "Well, I'm kind of traditional in that regard."

James laughed a little. It was enough to convince Marty that a resolution arrived.

"Go home and talk to your daughter, James," Marty said. "Believe me, if you sit down and tell her your concerns, all of them, even the ones that make you look weak, emotional, and fearful, she will listen. And then you have to do the same for her. But know that whatever decision you both make, it'll be the right one. Because wherever she is that night, she'll recognize the true meaning of Christmas."

James took a deep breath, extended his hand, and, after a manly shake, apologized for his behavior. He went home to follow Marty's advice.

While he resumed his Internet radio show, Marty chuckled to himself. He suddenly realized that at his age, he was a youth minister to just about everyone.

SAD

Faces Unknown

Lois sat in her room, surrounded by such delightful company!

It was a small space, so most of them stood. With the ease of a skilled debutante, Lois moved in and out of conversations with her visitors, careful to never end a discussion until her conversationalist had sparked a new dialogue with someone else. The space buzzed with adults' hearty, jocular banter. The lone child among them sat in one of the two available chairs—the other chair still empty—remaining silent and appearing quite agitated.

Between idle chit-chat with her company, Lois looked at the pouting little girl and said, "I promise, just as soon as they leave, we'll go out and have fun. I love to play just as much as you do, remember? But we mustn't be rude to our friends."

Just then, a set of knuckles gently rapped upon Lois' door.

"Come in," Lois sang over the drone of her gathering.

A woman far older than any of Lois' other visitors and who looked to be well past seventy entered the room, saying, "Hello, Lois. How are you today?"

"I'm marvelous, thank you for asking! Please, don't mind the crowd; come in and take a seat."

With a slight look of discomfort upon her face, the new guest made her way to the nearest chair.

"Oh, no! Not there!" Lois called out, losing her composure. "You don't want to sit on my little friend, do you? Please, use the other chair, the empty one."

The woman, seemingly mortified, quickly planted herself in the other chair. Lois realized the room had gone silent. She looked to everyone and said, "Now, it was an honest mistake! No harm, no foul!" Lois smiled when the din of lively chatter promptly resumed.

"So," Lois initiated, "do you know everyone here? I'd be happy to introduce you to whomever you wish."

The visitor's eyes darted away from Lois before she said, "I'm afraid I don't know who's with you at the moment."

"Not to worry, dear. I'm happy to help with faces unknown. For instance, if you look over your shoulder, you'll see Max Beasley. Can you believe he asks me to marry him nearly every time he visits? I'm not sure how much longer I can keep him at bay. Though he wouldn't be such a bad catch, you know. His father owns the corner gas station. Gasoline seems to be a lucrative industry."

Looking over her shoulder half-heartedly, the most recent guest returned her gaze to Lois and said, "I knew a man by the name of Max Beasley once, but he was much older than the person you're describing."

"Oh?" Lois mused. "Perhaps the person you know is a relative or something. Maybe that's where Max got his name. I'll have to ask him later." Lois then said, "What about Captain Marlow over there? I'm sure you'd love his tales of navigating the Congo River. He keeps promising to ferry me one day himself, but I have such motion sickness, I don't believe I could stand it! I've never been one for nautical travel."

"Actually," the woman said, "I came to see you, Lois."

"Me?"

"Yes."

Lois, in a display of uncommon anxiety, wrung her hands. She studied the woman as politely as possible, then, after a defeated sigh, said, "My dear, I'm afraid I simply can't place your face. Have we met?"

"Several times. But, please, don't worry about it. My name is Angelica Black."

Angelica reached out her hand and Lois shook it with a bright smile spread across her countenance.

"Do you hear that, Angie?" Lois asked as she addressed the little girl, lower lip still protruding. "This nice woman has the same name as you! What an interesting coincidence."

Angelica mustered all her strength and offered a soft, amiable laugh.

"Angie and I were just getting ready, once our guests leave, to go play at Shallow Creek. Do you know it?"

"I know it like an old friend," Angelica replied.

Lois and Angelica discussed Shallow Creek, as well as many other local areas of adventurous interests, at great length. Lois had to frequently remind Angie to remain patient, that they would be on

their way to play soon, but Angie, judging by Lois'
reactions, grew more and more impetuous.

Finally, feeling that she had asked more from a
little girl than anyone should, Lois genially requested
her guests return at a later time, that she had
neglected Angie for far too long, and, in truth, Lois
was just as itchy to splash in Shallow Creek's waters
as was her young friend.

Lois stood to escort her callers from out of her
room, and Angelica lingered so as to be the last to
leave—discounting Angie, of course.

Finally, once satisfied everyone else had gone,
Lois warmly waved her arm in a gesture for Angelica
to also exit.

Angelica said, "You must love your time at
Shallow Creek."

"Oh, I do," Lois said. "But it's really Angie's
company I value so. She's the best friend I've ever
had, to be quite honest. The age discrepancy is really
no matter. I can always be myself around her, and
she never belittles my extravagances. I thank God I
have her in my life."

"I'm sure she's just as thankful for you, Lois,"
Angelica said with her eyes threatening to overflow.

Lois furrowed her brow as though slightly confused, cordially smiled, and then Angelica watched as her lifelong friend closed the door to an empty room.

"Hello, Mrs. Black," Nurse Nash greeted as Angelica walked by. "My shift just started, and I haven't yet seen Mrs. Beasley. How is she today?"

Angelica, her cheeks wet, returned, "Lois is with her best friend. She couldn't be happier."

Pacified

Rick watched his seven-year-old daughter play on the equipment with several children she did not know. Rick didn't know them either, though they presumably belonged to his coworkers. During the ten years he'd been with Exisson Technology Solutions, this marked the first time they held a corporate cookout at a reserved park. All three hundred employees were required to attend, as were, if possible, their families. Rick's wife had to work a shift that evening, but he was able to bring his daughter. Personnel were expected to sit at randomly assigned plastic banquet tables.

While he kept an eye on his daughter, he listened to the surrounding chatter.

"The guy's a total idiot," Blake asserted.

Elena agreed, saying, "I have no idea how he got hired in the first place."

"He can't be that bad," Blake's wife, Lila, offered.

"Oh, he is," Elena said. "Bad coach. Bad employee. Bad everything."

Blake and Elena had daughters the same age. They played in a league called Tomorrow's Greatest Stars Today Soccer League, or TGSTSL. Their coworker, Vernon, also had an eleven-year-old daughter, and he happened to coach the very team on which Blake and Elena's children played.

Blake criticized, "He's only coaching so his daughter will get playing time."

Elena laughed, adding, "That's the only way she'd get on the field. I bet the kid weighs more than me!"

Rick glanced at Elena.

Cassandra, a third workmate of Rick's, asked, "Did you just call Vernon's kid fat? That's hilarious!"

"Honey," Cassandra's fiancé began, "I don't think calling a child fat is—"

After a frigid look from Cassandra, he stopped speaking. Elena was Cassandra's supervisor, and Cassandra previously made it very clear to her betrothed that he should not contradict, belittle, or otherwise embarrass her in front of management.

Blake said, "We know where she gets it, right? Vernon is a heart attack waiting to happen. I bet his wife is a heifer, too."

Lila slapped Blake on the arm with a conspiratorial smile. Blake then turned his attention to Rick, asking, "What do you think, Rick? You're not saying much."

Turning to regard Blake, Rick replied, "I don't know Vernon very well."

Elena asked, "Why do you keep looking over there?"

"My daughter," Rick answered while pointing to the playground. "Lot of people at this park. Just keeping an eye on her. She's only seven."

"She should play with my Agnes," Elena said. "Agnes is a wonderful babysitter. She babysits all the time and the families she babysits for say she's better than even their college babysitters."

Without facing Elena, Rick mumbled, "I'll keep that in mind."

Blake returned to his favorite subject, saying, "You know we should have won last Saturday's game. Vernon's daughter let the ball go right by her."

Elena added, "She had no business playing goalie—not in the last quarter."

Rick noticed a wailing child who looked about four walking by them. She held her mother's hand while howling something about a puppy. The mother, a woman whom Rick recognized from human resources, ineffectively tried to console her with soothing words.

Once they passed, Elena hissed, "God, shut that crybaby up."

"Who cries at a party like this?" Cassandra asked. "A face painter, bouncy houses, an ice cream truck—they literally spared no expense."

"I bet this shindig cost as much as my annual salary," Blake griped. "They'll probably have to fire someone to recoup the cost."

"Let's hope it's Vernon," Elena quipped.

The mother and daughter seemed to be headed for the parking lot—leaving. They walked by the rock wall that Rick's daughter climbed. She stopped ascending in order to study the tearful girl.

Rick saw his daughter jump off the rock wall, run over to the slides, retrieve something from the woodchips, then sprint toward the parking lot. She yelled at the crying girl, but Rick couldn't make out what she said. Rick next witnessed the young girl and her mother halt, turn, and face his approaching daughter. Squinting his eyes, Rick perceived his

daughter hand the sobbing girl a tiny stuffed puppy.
The little girl screeched in joy. She reached out to hug
Rick's daughter, and though they didn't know each
other, Rick's daughter received the embrace with a
big smile. They parted. Rick's daughter joined a few
kids on the swings.

Blake tittered, then said, "Maybe if Vernon got
fired, he'd have to leave town and we could finally
start winning without his porker on the team."

If Rick had the same character as his daughter,
he would have told Blake, Elena, and Cassandra
exactly what he thought of them.

But he didn't.

Rick instead watched his daughter swing and
prayed that she would never change.

The Miscarried

Joseph wobbled through the backyard, jabbing his cane into the soft, grassy earth. His breath left in short, desperate gasps. Finally, he reached the tree at the back of his property. Fifty-three years ago, he planted it himself, alone, when it was but a sapling. Back then it had been vulnerable … tiny … and virtually unnoticeable. Likely, no one would have noticed had it disappeared.

Like Quinn disappeared.

But Joseph made sure it thrived. He covered it with sheets during the cold, buckets in the hail, chicken wire when the vermin were flush. He kept the neighborhood children away, made sure the lawn service men were careful, and decreed no pets could move within a twenty-foot radius.

For the first several years of the oak's life, Joseph spared no effort to thwart every dangerous factor imaginable. The oak had to persist at all costs.

He did for the tree what he could not do for Quinn.

Quinn.

Joseph flung his cane aside, dropped to his knees in front of the tree's wide base, and then placed his palms against it. His eyes closed as his head lowered.

He heard the birds singing above, the children playing at nearby houses, a mower a block away.

"Hello."

Joseph's eyes shot open and he craned his head toward the source of the sound. The sudden movement discombobulated his sense of balance, and he teetered sideways before a young man with the eyes of Joseph's wife gently took him by the shoulders and eased him to the plush turf.

Joseph whispered, "Quinn?"

"It's me."

Joseph's eyes glistened in the sunlight peeking through the oak's leaves. He gasped, "How?"

"A last request," Quinn replied. The smile he wore upon his face made Joseph's heart swell.

"I prayed ..." Joseph stammered, "... I prayed every night. Every night I prayed that I would get to see you ... at least once. I wanted nothing more ... It has been my ..."

"Your dying wish." Quinn took Joseph's hands in his own and said, "You don't have long."

"I understand," Joseph answered as he stared into Quinn's face. "That's why I came out here … I wanted to die next to you … your tree."

Quinn continued to smile, but Joseph noticed the young man's throat hitched a little.

"Most people," Quinn began, "they'd mourn, but they'd forget. You could have wished to see anyone—your wife, your other children, your own parents."

Shaking his head, Joseph replied, "I knew I'd see them again."

Quinn raised an eyebrow.

"I know, son. I know. I wanted to believe I'd see you, too, but I couldn't be sure. No one could tell me. I talked to our priest. I asked theology professors. I did everything I could to get an answer, but no one could give me one. So I prayed, and I wished, and I hoped for mercy."

"And now you have it," Quinn replied.

"You were a boy," Joseph chuckled. "Your mother was right."

"This is just how you've always imagined me."

Joseph lurched, grabbed his chest, and then eased forward into his child's arms. He said, "I loved you the moment I found out about you. I never stopped. Not once."

Quinn rested his chin atop Joseph's head, looked at a caterpillar upon a fallen leaf, and said, "I know."

Joseph leaned against the old oak, his heart finally at rest.

Stranglehold

I can't breathe.

All the time.

You hate me so much.

You hate me if I laugh too loud.

You hate me if I cry.

You hate me if I kneel.

You hate me if I march.

You hate me if I speak my mind.

You hate me if I don't want to talk.

You hate me if I'm smarter than you.

You hate me if I'm not smart enough.

You hate me if I look you in the eye.

You hate me if I turn my head.

You hate me if I live in the "bad" part of town.

You hate me if I'm your neighbor.

You hate me if I'm sitting on my porch.

You hate me if I'm at the park.

You hate me if I'm in my car, on the bus, or
riding the train.

You hate me if I'm walking somewhere.

You hate me if I'm rich.

You hate me if I'm poor.

You hate me if I go to college.

You hate me if I don't like school.

You hate me if I become your boss.

You hate me if I'm unemployed.

You hate me if I'm submissive.

You hate me if I fight.

You hate me if I win.

You hate me if I lose.

You hate me if I live.

You hate me if I die.

You hate me so much.

All the time.

I can't breathe.

Promise

"Why did I ask you to stay after class?"

"Because you're a punk."

"No, Sam. Try again."

Mr. Hardy could see the surprise on Sam's face. He figured that "punk" comment would get him sent straight to the office.

"… I don't know."

"I think you do. The test."

"What about it?"

"You played on your phone the whole time. You didn't answer a single question."

"I didn't read the book."

"Sam, we listened to it on audio as we read along. You at least *heard* it."

"Don't you have another class coming in or something?"

"No, this is my conference period. We've got plenty of time."

"I need to get to my next class."

"I'll write you a pass."

"Ms. Johnson gets pissed if students come in late without a pass. I don't want to be on her bad side."

"I'll write you a pass when we're done. I promise."

"Come on, Mr. Hardy. I need to go."

"Tell me why you didn't take the test, and then I'll let you go."

"I didn't know the answers."

"I watched you. You didn't even try the first page."

They both stood at the front of the class. Sam ran his hands up and down his backpack straps. He looked everywhere but at Mr. Hardy.

"Sam?"

"… There's no point."

"To what?"

"To the test."

"The test is how I assess your knowledge."

"I don't mean it like that. The test doesn't make any difference."

"Look, Sam, I know you're failing, but you're right on the edge. This test could put you over the top."

"You know I'm not going to graduate, right?"

"What? We're only halfway through the first semester. Of course you're going to graduate."

"No, I mean, I'm not going to graduate. Like, it's not going to happen."

"You're quitting school?"

"No."

"Sam … I'm confused. You're a senior on track to graduate."

"Can I go now?"

"No, Sam, I want to get to the bottom of this."

"You're being a total dick."

Sam locked eyes with Mr. Hardy. He hoped that one would send him to the principal.

"Call me whatever you want. We're having this conversation."

After throwing his head back, exasperated, Sam slid off his backpack and plopped down into a nearby desk. He took out his phone.

"You *can* graduate. It sounds like you're making a conscious decision *not* to graduate."

Sam scrolled with his finger. He left his earbuds out, though, so Mr. Hardy knew he had Sam's attention.

"Don't you want to graduate?"

"What's the point?"

"College. Junior college. Trade school. A job."

"I can't pay for college."

"There are scholarship opportunities, grants, that kind of thing."

"That's what you all keep telling me, but I don't know where to find that stuff."

"Our guidance counselors can help you. They want to help students take advantage of those things."

"Yeah. I went down there. Mr. Vonn found a few for me, sent me the links, then told me to come back when I looked at them."

"Did you look at them?"

"Yeah. I didn't know how to answer half the questions."

"Like what?"

"Like how much my mom makes in a year. How am I supposed to know that?"

"Did you ask her?"

Sam glared at Mr. Hardy like he was an idiot.

"Okay, how about we make arrangements for you to come in after school and I can sift through it with you. We can figure it out together. We'll ballpark those numbers they want."

"Then what?"

"Then we maybe get you into a junior college or trade school or something."

Sam didn't blink as he asked, "Then what?"

"Then you're off and running."

"You're serious?"

"I'm serious."

"What makes you think I know how to do college?"

"It's very similar to high school in terms of structure—"

"I've got friends at college. They say it's not like high school at all. I know a guy getting kicked out, and he's not even getting his money back."

"Well, that may be true. You have to maintain a certain grade point average. If you don't, they can make you leave."

"Nobody in my family has ever gone to college. I can't pay for it, I don't know how to do it, and I wouldn't fit in."

"I can help you with all that."

"Really? Are you going to be there for me the whole time? All four years?"

"I … I'll do my best. Of course, I have two kids of my own. This job demands a lot of my time as well. I can't promise—"

"Exactly. People like you love to make promises to people like me, but people like you never make good—not all the way through. People like me? We have to face reality."

"Which is?"

Sam emitted a chuckle. "The best I can hope for is some minimum wage job. That's my life, Mr. Hardy. That's what the future has in store for me. I'm always going to worry about food, rent, money— everything. I bet your kids have a nice house, a yard, their own bed. Hell, they probably even have their own bed*room.*"

"… They do."

"*Here*? I *like* it here. There's no one from the outside. I see my friends. The place is clean. There's food. The teachers can't mess with me. Why would I want to go out *there* when it's so good in *here*?"

"But … but your future …"

"… Look, can I go now or what?"

Mr. Hardy appeared dumbfounded. He whispered, "You're only a kid ..."

"Can I go now?"

Snapping back to attention, Mr. Hardy said, "Yeah. You can go."

Sam kept his phone in his one hand and snatched up his backpack with the other, then hustled out of the room.

"I forgot to write his pass."

Chubby Tummy

I remember standing in the shower with the steam rolling around me. The roar of the water combined with the whir of the fan created a loud, encapsulating experience. White stripes, each about the width of three fingers, stretched across the middle of the door just enough to shield one's private parts should someone enter the bathroom. In a house full of two adults and four children, such an invasion always proved likely. Even the dog committed the occasional incursion.

I remember staring at that clear glass with the white stripes. We once had a frosted glass door, but when my sister pushed it open too hard, it shattered. The shards fell everywhere and managed to slice open her forearm in the process. The neighbors put my two older siblings and me to bed that night because my parents drove her to the nearest emergency room, which was thirty minutes away.

I remember thinking my sister would not return home that night or any other night ever again.

I remember the beige stain that would appear on the floor of the shower. My mother made one of us scrub it every three days with bleach, but that brown residue never relented. With six people using one shower, Comet didn't stand a chance against the constant barrage of oil, dirt, and, in my case, urine.

I remember the metal drain in the center of the shower floor. At one time it appeared silver—a round, metallic plate with twenty-three holes. The drain had taken on a greenish tint, however, with a bit of blue mixed in. It reminded me of shipwrecks featured in those shows with strange sounding men who hunted undersea treasure. Bits of mashed Dial clung to the edges of the holes on the underside of the drain. When the soap wore down to a sliver and careened to the floor, we would press it against the drain until it pushed through like sausage in a grinder. We took my mother to the brink of insanity.

I remember all the bottles lining the perimeter of the shower stall. My mother and two sisters each had their own brand of shampoo and conditioner. My dad complained he barely had anywhere to stand because of all the plastic containers. Dad told my brother and me just to use the bar of soap for our hair, but I actually used my sisters' stuff. I would wash my hair every other day while making sure to switch from one brand to the next to the next. This method served me well for months until my oldest sister recognized her scent of raspberry atop my head during an impromptu wrestling match that resulted due to my unauthorized use of her athletic socks. As the youngest member of the family, I mastered the art of scavenging in order to fulfill my needs.

I remember looking down in the shower to see my tummy blocking the view of my toes. The hot water hit the back of my head and flowed downward. It caught my dark hair in its currents and pushed my bangs into my eyes. I saw black tendrils hovering over a pink balloon—my fat gut.

I remember hating myself.

I remember my sisters, my brother, my father and mother—they were slender, toned, slim, strong. You could actually see my brother's muscles through the skin of his stomach. I didn't understand. My legs were lean, as were my arms. But my face carried a lot of flab in the jowls and my stomach—it looked like someone blew up a beach ball inside of me.

I remember being so confused. We all ate the same foods, drank the same drinks. Why were they so skinny? Why was I the only tubby member of my family? To make matters worse, it seemed like I got fatter every day. Wasn't it bad enough that I regularly got the lowest grades amongst my siblings? Didn't the world beat me up enough in that I always got picked last for sports? My oldest sister earned multiple academic scholarships—colleges lined up for her approval. My older brother consistently won the lead in every school play through elementary, middle, and high school. My other sister, though only a year older than me, could outplay anyone at soccer. Everyone agreed the Olympics could be in her future. Me? I could eat twice as much bread at dinner as my entire family combined. That was my only claim to fame.

I remember feeling hopeless. My grandmother once called me chunky when we hosted Thanksgiving. She said I inherited it from her side of the family. After her proclamation, I slowly and inconspicuously backed away from the table before fleeing to the room I shared with my brother. I sobbed for an hour before my mother found me. She tried to assure me that I would thin out. She compared me to a squirrel saving up for the winter. According to her, I would soon hit a growth spurt. This sudden growth would burn up all of my blubber as I got taller and taller.

I remember thinking that sounded like bullshit.

I remember looking down at my gut in the shower. It would glisten like raw chicken meat as the hot, soapy water streamed over it. It stuck out so far that I couldn't even see my thing. My best friends were thin as could be. We ate the same food at lunch—why weren't they fat? Pudding pies, Twinkies, Nutty Bars, Swiss Cake Rolls, Cosmic Brownies—we all ate them! They drank Coke just like me, too.

I remember wondering if I would always be fat. Would I just get fatter and fatter? Would my arms and legs start to swell as well? Was I eternally destined to be the beefy kid? Would girls like me? Would I ever find someone willing to marry me? What would PE class be like for the rest of my life? Would coaches keep teasing me worse and worse, year after year? Would my dad's friends ever stop accusing me of sneaking beer? Would the middle school kids bully me? Would people laugh at me until the day I died?

I remember standing in the steaming, noisy shower while praying to God to make my chubby gut disappear before sixth grade.

Crisis

"He's dying, damn it, and he's all alone!"

"Mom—he's not alone."

Holly looked at her nineteen-year-old daughter through narrowed eyes. She held her cell phone in both hands after hanging up with the hospital as she stood next to the kitchen island.

"He's not alone? Abby, *what* are you talking about?" Holly demanded.

Just a few feet away, standing by the kitchen table, Abby put her own cell phone down and replied, "Dad's not alone—you know that."

"Really?" Holly seethed with her head tilted. "Who's with him, then?"

Abby answered, "Jesus."

Throwing her chin back, Holly groaned, "Christ almighty."

After folding her arms, Abby declared, "Exactly."

Holly stomped past her daughter before plopping down on the living room couch. With her elbows upon her knees, she dropped her head into her hands.

Abby did not move from her spot, nor did she unfold her arms. She questioned, "You know that, right?"

Holly murmured into her palms, "Yes, I know. But your father needs more than that. He needs *us*."

Abby lifted her eyebrows just a bit as she asked, "He needs us more than *Jesus*? Before the coma, when they kicked everyone out of the hospital, Dad texted me. He said he wasn't afraid. He cited Psalm 23."

Holly lifted her head up and stared at her daughter. "I really don't want to hear about the valley of Death right now, okay?"

"Are you worried about him?" Abby asked.

"What's the matter with you?" Holly spat. "Yes, I'm worried about him! The doctor said he's not going to make it!"

"But Dad's okay with that," Abby said as she unfolded her arms and shrugged her shoulders. "He *wants* to go to Heaven. That's what we all want, right?"

"God," Holly mumbled. "You go off to college and become a theology expert …"

"No," Abby answered coldly. "I'm not a theology expert; I'm just repeating everything *you* taught me. What's the matter with *you*?"

Holly jumped from the couch, pointed at Abby, and screamed, "Your father is dying! My husband is dying—alone, in a coma, suffocating—and nobody cares! Our own daughter doesn't care!"

Abby put her hands on her hips and took a deep breath. Once she had control, she said, "I care. I care very much. But you *and* Dad taught me to believe, to have faith, and to accept Christ into my heart. You taught me to do these things so we could one day reach Heaven and join Him in all His glory. Are you saying you don't actually believe those things?"

Holly fell to her knees and began to cry. Between sobs, she said, "Those are just things we tell kids … children's stories …"

Abby stood her ground. "That's not true. Not to me. Not to Dad."

Unable to meet her daughter's eyes, Holly remained on her knees with her head hung low.

"I don't understand you," Abby confessed. "You were our youth group sponsor. We prayed together every dinner—every night before bed. You got me up every Sunday for church. I don't …"

"Those things …" Holly began as she fought to stifle her tears, "… they were just the right thing to do. I wanted to raise you … right."

With eyes widened, Abby asked, "Are you saying you never actually believed?"

Holly faced her daughter again. Tears ran down her cheeks and her throat hitched. As she started to answer, Abby interrupted her.

"Don't," Abby said. "Don't say anything. You don't have to answer."

Abby moved toward her mother, dropped to her knees as well, and wrapped her arms around her.

The daughter placed her head atop the mother's and squeezed tightly.

"You're upset. No matter what, I know Jesus is sitting with Dad right now, holding his hand. And Dad knows it, too. He's not afraid. He's joyful."

Holly whispered, "I hope you're right."

The two women remained on the floor, hugging one another, waiting for the call.

Together

The father sat next to his three-year-old son, listening to the steady pulse of the heart monitor. The Hospice nurses said the device would be unnecessary, but he insisted.

Though his boy, Tommy, no longer experienced consciousness, the father kept the pillow pet turned on, as well as the nightlight that shot a Batman image upon the ceiling. Various stuffed animals surrounded his child, just the way he would arrange them back before …

The father kept vigil all night and all day. A countdown commenced last week; he would not leave his son's side. He quit his job, stopped paying his bills, ceased answering calls and texts. He allowed Hospice entrance, as well as his own parents and Maggie's parents, but beyond that he admitted no one.

Maggie.

Tommy kept a picture of them on his nightstand—Maggie and the father. The child demanded as such after moving out of the crib. They allowed it because, frankly, it kept him in bed and helped him fall asleep, which made their lives a lot easier.

The picture remained in place, but the father wanted to shatter the frame and rip the photograph to shreds. Every time he looked at it. Every time he looked at her.

He hated her.

Loathe her as he did, he understood her desertion. She couldn't bear to witness her baby waste away and die, so she fled. He wanted to do the same. He felt no desire to wait for Death.

But Tommy needed him. Tommy needed him since the moment of birth—needed fed, changed, washed, clothed—and the father not once shirked his responsibilities. Now would be no different. Now, when Tommy needed him more than ever, the father had no intention of letting down his son.

That's the difference between the father and mother. And that's why he hated her. That's why he would never forgive her.

A Precious Moments cross hung above the light switch near the door. It blatantly mocked the father. Once Maggie left, he wanted to take it down, but his own parents begged him to leave it. The father did not believe in God, despite having been raised by devout parents, but Maggie did. He believed when Tommy died, that would be the end of it. There did not exist an afterlife. Heaven was but a fairy tale parents told children to make them feel better about grandparents dying.

But he couldn't risk being wrong.

Once, at the splash park, a little boy of Tommy's size, build, and hair color wore the exact same trunks. Though the father stood in the shallow water near Tommy, he looked away briefly to say hello to a friend, and when he returned his watchful eye to the boy, moments passed before he realized the subject of his attention was not his son at all—it was the other boy. Absolute panic invaded the father's mind. He lost all rationality, his pulse thrummed, his ears pounded. Darting his eyes around, he soon located Tommy. The toddler waddled toward his mother. The father laughed, joined his wife and son, and informed them that he'd been tricked by Tommy's doppelganger. The mother smiled and told the father she'd been watching Tommy the whole time, there was no need for alarm.

Maggie was a great mom when it was easy to be a great mom.

When the doctors told them Tommy's … cancer … could not be reversed or cured, that it would kill the child within months, the father suffered a reaction far more potent than that brief moment at the pool. The thought of his son, alone, horrified him. Tommy would never be abandoned in life, nor would he be forsaken in death.

He stroked Tommy's mound of tussled hair. The doctor convinced them that chemotherapy, in this case, would only torture the child—it would momentarily delay the inevitable while lessening Tommy's quality of life in the duration. The father did not want Tommy's last months spent in the hospital. The mother offered no input for she had, by that point, mentally checked out. She soon physically followed suit.

The heart monitor stopped its cadence and instead emitted a shrill tune. The father glanced at the cross and cursed. He then unplugged the device.

The father pulled out the note he'd kept in his pocket for months. It needed to be available at a moment's notice. He next took out the case he also kept at the ready.

He needed something fast, clean, and relatively painless. Propofol gained notoriety years ago after killing Michael Jackson. It was extraordinarily easy to buy off the street. He filled the syringe. He plunged the needle into his arm.

As he embraced his son, the father whispered, "I'm here."

FUNNY

A Blind Date for a New Year

Ellen Knowles entered the posh restaurant, shook the snow from her black Rivington leather boots, removed her pink cashmere wrap, and then approached the thin-faced, large-bellied maître d'.

"Happy New Year, Madame!" he exclaimed in perfectly rehearsed passion.

"Soon enough, I hope," she replied without looking at him. She unbuttoned her overcoat.

"How may I be of service, Madame?" he asked as he admired her immaculate wardrobe.

"I'm meeting someone; perhaps he's here already?"

"Ah, yes," the maître d' purred with a smile full of jagged white pebbles. "You must speak of Mr. McLeay. He said a ravishing woman might arrive in search of a rendezvous. Follow me, if you please."

Ellen trailed the maître d', ignoring the fact that the tails of his tuxedo remained inert due to his rotund posterior. Finally, she perceived a lone man wearing a rather shabby brown sport coat. He sat at a table dressed in white cloth with two lit candles upon it. Tiny flames danced along the man's forehead as he perspired.

"Hi," he said upon noticing her approach. He rose from his seat and offered an unadorned hand. "You must be Ellen."

"I am," she said as she gracefully—and rather slowly—removed her black leather gloves. She finally took his still hovering hand within her own and, after realizing that he intended only to shake it, said, "And you must be Bartholomew."

"Lord! Please—call me Bart. Bartholomew makes me feel like I'm back in grade school."

She smiled, her red lips dazzling in the soft light surrounding them, and assured, "Then 'Bart' it shall be."

Ellen remained upright as Bart took his seat in an effort to hide his frumpy black pants from her sight. She waited a few moments as he readjusted his silverware, eyes darting between her and the cutlery, then removed her own black wool Bella overcoat. Though the establishment achieved a pleasing ambiance and reputedly served exquisite cuisine, Ellen found their lack of a coat check service deplorable.

She positioned her outerwear over the back of her chair in order to avoid any potential wrinkles before seating herself.

"I'm glad a meeting could finally be arranged. Anderson had wonderful things to say about you," she commented while grasping the corners of her dinner napkin. She flung it onto her lap with an efficiency that would render Martha Stewart envious.

Bart snatched up his napkin sprawled upon the table, fought the urge to stuff it into the collar of his plaid shirt, and instead tossed it onto his right leg. "He said great things about you, too. Though, I have to say, he didn't tell me you were quite so ..."

Bart trailed off and averted her gaze.

Ellen's brown eyes grew slightly wide, and, had she been a less polished woman, might even have lifted her eyebrows in anticipation. When it became obvious that Bart would rather play with his salad fork than conclude his statement, she pressed the matter.

"He didn't tell you I was quite so *what*, Bart?" she requested pleasantly enough, though her pulse quickened.

Bart finally allowed his salad fork some time alone, glanced up at her, and said, "Aw, Ellen, I hate to be so forward. I can only imagine what you must be thinking right now, so I better come out with it. I have a habit of sticking my foot in my mouth, you see, and even though it's been a long time, I don't remember being too impressive on first dates, especially on such an important day ..."

"It's only New Year's Eve, Bart. It's not so very important."

At the conclusion of Ellen's statement, Bart's face seemed to take on a mixture of both ash and crimson. He felt a blind date on New Year's Eve could only be outranked by a date on one's birthday or Christmas itself!

"You were saying, Bart?"

"Oh, right. Well, Ellen, what I was about to say, before I worried about being too direct, you see, is that Anderson didn't tell me, well, he didn't tell me you were so—forgive me, Ellen—but he didn't tell me you were so *beautiful*."

Though her posture remained pristine, Ellen's heart rate tripled and she couldn't help but smile ... a little. She leaned almost imperceptibly forward, so as not to be judged a tart by any of the establishment's eavesdropping connoisseurs, and replied, "Nor did Anderson tell *me* you were so very handsome."

A wide smile spread across Bart's face.

Inching ever closer toward her date—meddlesome eavesdroppers be damned—Ellen divulged, "I lied, Bart. A blind date on New Year's Eve is very special indeed, and though I struggled against my family's discovery of this engagement, Anderson found it humorous to email all of them with the news."

Laughter erupted from Bart's depths, and he confessed, "That fool did the same thing to me, too! I bet I'll have at least four different messages on my voice mail tonight."

The server at last arrived and set a menu before both Ellen and Bart. "Shall we perhaps begin with a glass of wine, Madame and Monsieur?"

Ellen perused the menu, as did Bart; however, because she was so absorbed in the restaurant's delicious selection, she didn't notice his eyes bulge when he read the outrageous prices.

Returning her attention to the waitress, Ellen asked, "Before we order, I must inquire: Do you honor AARP discounts?"

"Of course, Madame, though we do require a membership card."

Looking across the elegant dinner table, Ellen asked, "How about it, Bart? Did you bring your card tonight?"

His heart fought to free itself from the confines of his chest as Bart answered, "You bet your boots, Ellen."

"Very good, then," Ellen said to the server. "We'll start with a bottle of Dom Pérignon Rose."

Bart praised, "You're my kind of woman, Ellen."

Despite all her refined inclinations, Ellen winked in return.

A Man, His Wife, and His Comics

Karen looked at me, cocked her head, offered a smile, then said, "What are you doing with your comics?"

Six years ago, we built a house together. We didn't actually build it, of course, I can barely wield a hammer, but we worked together, man and wife, to make every infinite decision that goes into literally making a home.

We picked an empty lot in a nice subdivision close to a good school and promptly told our builder to give us the absolute minimum square footage the covenants allowed. He vowed that while our home would not be the biggest, it would be the most charming. We felt like he kept his end of the bargain.

Because we saved for many years, we could afford the house and still retain a nice sum in our bank account, but only if we left the basement unfinished. Though we both loved basements, we knew that particular feat would have to be accomplished another day.

Two children were born in the interim, Elizabeth and baby Loraine, and suddenly our small but charming home proved effectively too constricting. The time to tackle the basement had finally arrived.

Now in our mid-thirties, refinancing our mortgage didn't turn out to be too troublesome; it actually worked to our advantage. We interviewed a cavalcade of contractors, picked the one my wife clicked with the most, signed the paperwork, and now … now the time occurred to clear out all the junk we amassed during the last six years.

It's amazing how an unfinished basement essentially becomes a storage unit. Got something you don't want seen on the main level? Toss it in the basement. Stuff piling up down there? No worries, you'll clean it out later, like when you decide to finish the basement. Oops.

DVDs, CDs, VHS tapes—donated to charity. Decrepit chairs, damaged end tables, faulty lamps—to the curb! The contractor gave us a start date merely fifteen days away, so we purged with impunity as we fought against the clock.

All proceeded swimmingly until we reached seven plastic containers. They were long and thin, meant to fit under a bed. I had them stacked upon each other in a corner and camouflaged by folding chairs and card tables.

So, when Karen questioned my intentions regarding the comic book collection, I hesitated not at all when saying, "I'll probably put them in the guest room closet."

Her face told me I answered incorrectly.

"Sweetie," she began, "maybe it's time to sell them?"

"Oh, most of them are worthless."

Confusion spread across her face. She thought for a few moments, apparently calculating how best to respond. She must have decided when dealing with me the direct approach worked best, so she simply asked, "If they're worthless, why are you keeping them?"

"Well, I've always had them."

"Okay, but you don't collect comics anymore, do you?"

She got me there. I mean, I still bought collected editions of comics, generally called graphic novels even though that's a bit of a misnomer. I displayed those books proudly on my shelves among favorite novelists like Auster, Chabon, and Proulx. But as far as the single-issue comic books? No, I hadn't bought one of those in years.

"Why do you want me to get rid of them?" I asked rather bluntly.

"We need the space."

"Okay, instead of the guest room closet, I'll put them under our bed."

"What if I don't want them under our bed?"

"Why wouldn't you want them under our bed?" I asked.

"You're seriously asking a grown woman why she doesn't want 5,000 comic books stored under her bed?"

She had a point.

"You have a point," I replied.

Opting for a change in stratagem, she asked, "Could you just keep the ones that are valuable? *Are* any of them valuable?"

"Probably. I mean, I have Bane's first appearance—that's probably worth something, right?"

"Who's Bane?"

I snapped my fingers before saying, "I've also got the first issue of Wolverine's first ever solo series.

I bet that's worth something. That's gotta be worth something!"

Karen placed her hands on her hips. She obviously struggled to retain patience. I'd seen that same body language used with our children.

She said, "I have trouble believing they're that important if you don't even know how much they're worth."

"Well, I mean, monetarily speaking, I have no idea how much they're worth."

"Monetarily speaking?" she repeated.

"Yeah, even though most of them are from the '80s and '90s, they're worth a ton to me. They're special. They were with me the whole time I was a kid."

"You were happy as a kid!" she exclaimed.

"I know, but when I think of my childhood, they're there. I mean, I vividly remember reading my Todd McFarlane *Spider-Man* comics when they came in the mail—my first subscription! I remember my babysitter, Janie Myer, buying me my first comic book at her dad's gas station—it was a *World's Finest*. I can dig it out if you want ..."

"That won't be necessary."

"I remember reading about Kyle Rayner taking over as Earth's Green Lantern the night my grandpa died. I mean, when I think of my past, I think of them. They're like, anchors, to who I was, where I was, even how I became who I am now."

"But you never look at them anymore," she reminded. "I can't remember the last time you got them out."

I walked across the room and took Karen in my arms. While I hugged her tightly, I said, "I stopped buying comics when I met you. When I think of the last eleven years, you are in every single one of my memories. When I think of the last four years, the girls are in every single one of my memories, too. My childhood ended, in a good way, when I met you, but I don't want to completely leave it behind. You guys are the most special people in my life now, but those comics remind me of a lot of special people also, you know?"

Karen hugged me harder as she huffed, "You're *still* a child, you know that, right?"

"I know."

"Fine," she groaned while letting go of me and walking away. "I have to go pick up the girls. Start moving those things up to the guest room, okay? They're not going under my bed."

My heart leapt as I answered, "You bet."

Climbing the stairs, she called, "Those special people you mentioned?"

"Yeah?"

"They're Batman and Superman, aren't they?"

I kept quiet on that one.

Healthy Balls

"Peas is a silly name," said eight-year-old Elise. "It sounds kind of yucky, you know, like …"

"Pee-pee!" exclaimed Elise's four-year-old sister, Loretta.

"Come on, now, enough of that," Steve said as he sat down at the table.

"Sorry," Loretta mumbled.

"No, you're not," Elise chided.

"I'm not!" Loretta bellowed before laughing maniacally.

"All right," Caroline interrupted, "your father made your favorite. Let's eat while it's hot."

Loretta roared, "Bow tie pasta! Yum!"

"Glad somebody's excited for it," Steve chuckled.

Steve did indeed make the girls' favorite dinner. The night previous, he'd made meatloaf, never a popular choice among his children, but a favorite of his wife's. He thought tonight he'd make something they'd all enjoy. Of course, Elise and Loretta eat the mini farfalle with only Alfredo sauce, whereas he and his wife add peas, red pepper, green pepper, onion, and Parmesan. Steve takes it even a step further with small Italian sausage slices. Not to worry, the girls must still eat their peas, albeit in a separate dish with too much butter.

Obviously, the peas were a topic of great concern to Elise.

"Don't you think 'peas' is kind of a weird name?" Elise asked anyone willing to answer.

"I guess," Caroline replied.

Elise grinned, and said, "Yeah, like when I drop a pea on the floor, I have to say, 'Oops, I pead on the floor.'"

Loretta erupted.

"I don't think I've ever heard it phrased quite like that," Steve added.

"No, Steve, she's right," Caroline said. "It does sound a little funny to warn people, 'Oh, no! Don't step in my pea!'"

Steve groaned, "Seriously? You're doing it, too?"

The girls burst out laughing, so hard, in fact, that Loretta very nearly fell out of her seat. Steve caught her by the shoulder and hefted her back up into place.

"What would be a better alternative?" Caroline asked Elise.

"Huh?"

Caroline clarified, "What would be a better name for peas?"

Elise took a bite of her garlic bread and thought for several moments. After great contemplation, she finally revealed, "I've got it! Green balls!"

Caroline took a drink of soda the moment Elise said this, and within an instant she had to cover her mouth to keep from spitting it out.

Loretta noticed her mother, started pointing, and shouted, "Look at Mommy! Look at Mommy!"

"Green balls, huh?" Steve repeated. "I've got to be honest, kiddo … that doesn't sound appetizing."

Finally under control, Caroline giggled, "I mean, it's already hard enough to get most kids to eat their peas, you know? I'm not sure calling them 'green balls' will get children excited for a big spoonful."

"Not me, that's for sure," Steve said.

"But you don't eat peas, Daddy," Loretta enlightened.

"True enough, sweetheart," he answered.

Elise, a thoughtful young girl, took the matter to heart. "So, we need a name that will make kids want to eat peas but not sound like, you know …"

"Pee-pee!" Loretta hollered. "Pee-pee! Pee-pee!"

"We got it, Loretta," Caroline said with a smile.

"And 'green balls' isn't any good?" she tested again.

Steve finished chewing before saying, "I won't lie—it's not great."

"Okay. Well then … how about … healthy balls!"

Caroline's eyes closed so tightly that they began to water as she hunched over and tried her hardest not to laugh. Instead, a sequence of rasps escaped accompanied by a strange series of heaving and jostling.

"I think that's perfect, Elise," Steve said. "The doctors will love it. I mean, 'healthy balls.' It sounds very nutritious."

"You think so?" Elise asked. "It's good?"

Caroline, still unable to talk as she fought to contain her laughter, offered her husband a silent warning with a quick shake of her head.

"It's very good," Steve agreed. "I think everyone should have healthy balls."

"It doesn't sound gross?" Elise questioned.

"Only if there's a hair on them," her father added.

"Steve!" Caroline chastised.

"No, Daddy's right," Elise confirmed. "If I find a hair on my food, I can't eat anymore. It totally grosses me out."

"Okay," Caroline began after finally having composed herself, "let's change topics."

"Why?" Loretta asked.

"Yeah, why?" Steve repeated with an ornery grin.

"I think kids would love healthy balls," Elise informed.

"I think we all would," Steve added. "People will grab big handfuls."

Caroline again lost control. She pressed her eyes shut, pursed her lips, and tried with all her might to keep it together.

"Maybe Daddy will like to eat them now!" Loretta said.

"Hmm. I don't know, Lo," Steve said. "I mean, it is just a name change. I'm guessing they would still taste the same. I'd have to ask someone to try them out for me. Maybe your mom would do me a favor and taste my healthy balls?"

At this Caroline screeched, "Excuse me!" before racing to the bathroom. They heard her slam the door, turn on the fan, run the water, and then emit a sound so jarring that the girls' eyes grew quite concerned.

"Is Mommy crying?" Loretta asked.

It'd been a while since Steve heard such a ruckus from his wife. He informed the girls, "Ladies, what you're hearing is your mother's genuine laughter. It is not for the weak of heart."

Elise looked at Steve very seriously and said, "I don't think you guys are talking about peas."

Loretta added, "I think they're talking about real balls!"

Steve then had to excuse himself from the table as well.

Some time passed before the parents rejoined their children, at which point they agreed they should probably stick with the name "peas" and have no more talk of healthy balls.

Loretta, however, noticed Steve and Caroline's conspiratorial glance to one another. She offered one of her own to Elise, which prompted a mischievous smirk in return.

This was not over.

Over My Dead Body

As Preston, Jared, Reggie, and Dale snuck out of Reggie's car and slithered among the shadows of the sidewalk to Mr. Washington's house, Jared said, "I heard Andy ratted us out, guys. They're saying Washington bribed him with doughnuts."

Reggie replied, "So what if he did? Look, Mr. Washington's house is completely dark. He's probably in bed by now."

"I bet he doesn't even hand out candy to trick-or-treaters," Preston laughed.

"He just gives them math problems to solve," Dale added.

"Well," Reggie began, "he's definitely getting a trick tonight!"

The boys, hunched over like covert operatives, glided through Mr. Washington's yard. Jared and Dale veered off past the weeping willow and started jabbing plastic fork after plastic fork into the well-kept grass while Preston and Reggie broke out the plastic wrap and headed for the driveway and Mr. Washington's prized possession—a 1955 red and white Crown Victoria.

"We should have brought toilet paper," Preston whispered as he moved to the opposite side of the car.

"Nah, it's been done," Reggie said. "Man, I can't wait to see old Washington's face Monday morning. We're going to be legends after this!"

Stabbing one fork after another into the cool ground, Dale glanced over and saw Preston and Reggie tightly wrapping the car. "This is awesome!" he whispered to Jared. "No one's ever been able to pull a prank on Mr. Washington!"

Jared grinned and returned, "Looks like there's a first time for everything."

Just then, Mr. Washington erupted from the front porch while flinging eggs at the boys and yelling, "You scoundrels! What took you so long? I've been waiting for you all night!"

With yolk oozing down this forehead, Dale screamed, "Run! Andy snitched!"

But then Mr. Washington tripped over his last step and landed hard on the front walk.

Broken eggs surrounded his inert body.

Preston, Reggie, Jared, and Dale all laughed … until they realized he wasn't getting up. Knowing their teacher's reputation for deception, they gingerly approached.

Even in the dark, they saw something amiss.

"Oh, my—is that blood?" Dale asked beneath his breath.

Preston said, "Turn his body over so we can see his face."

"No!" Reggie exclaimed. "Never move someone who's unconscious."

"We should call an ambulance," Dale said.

Jared demanded, "He's face down in his own blood, guys—we have to move him or he could choke to death!"

"If he's not already dead," Dale added.

"Shut up with that!" Reggie admonished.

Preston knelt beside his felled teacher. He took Mr. Washington by the shoulders and rolled him over.

Jared said, "I'll turn on my flashlight so we can see how bad he's hurt."

Once illuminated, Mr. Washington's face, implausibly injured, horrified his students.

Reggie uttered, "We killed him."

"We're going to jail," Preston muttered after turning away from the sight.

Jared, his voice shaking, whimpered, "But it wasn't our fault!"

Suddenly, the boys saw the porch lights flare to life as Mrs. Washington shrieked, "Noah? Noah? What happened?"

The boys could not move when Mrs. Washington rushed down the porch steps and hurled herself upon her husband's body.

With tear-stained cheeks, she looked up and wailed, "What did you do? What did you do to my darling Noah?"

Lifting his palms up in surrender, Jared cried, "Nothing! He just fell! We didn't touch him!"

Mr. Washington abruptly sprang to unnatural life, dragged his wife to the ground, and appeared to seize her jugular with his front teeth.

Blood spurted from Mrs. Washington's neck even as she begged for mercy.

Jared and Dale did not hesitate. They bolted.

Reggie and Preston remained, but when they saw Mrs. Washington go limp and Mr. Washington face them with blood dripping down his chin, they quickly followed suit.

Mr. Washington's bestial roars gave way to uncontrollable laughter.

"Are they gone?" Mrs. Washington asked while sitting up and wiping the fake blood from her neck.

"They're gone," Mr. Washington guffawed. "You did great, honey!"

Mrs. Washington looked at her husband and said, "How I let you talk me into this foolishness is beyond me. That's the last time you use my supplies for these silly pranks of yours."

"Fair enough," Mr. Washington said before giving his wife a messy peck on the cheek. "I can't wait to see those jokers' faces Monday morning when they walk into class and see me standing there."

No longer able to resist laughing as well, Mrs. Washington smiled and said, "Well, this was one of your best, I'll give you that. You'll never outgrow these things, will you?"

"What? And give *them* the upper hand? Over my dead body!"

Mrs. Washington put her arm around her husband's waist, shook her head, and then ascended the porch steps with him.

"What do you say we leave the lights on for the trick-or-treaters?" Mr. Washington asked.

"Isn't it too late for that? There shouldn't be anyone out at this hour."

"Oh," Mr. Washington sang, "there are always a few stragglers. Just this once, I think I'll reward tardiness."

Mrs. Washington almost asked if her husband would like to clean the gruesome make-up off his face before handing out candy, but she knew better than to bother.

Follow Me

"TJ, wake up!"

TJ rolled over, reached down to the outlet, and flipped on his race car nightlight. His grandmother must have turned it off at some point after he fell asleep. His room suddenly illuminated in a weak blanket of light. Brent had done this exact same thing to him a few weeks before, so TJ fully expected an encore of the rubber Wolfman mask glaring at him again. This time, though, TJ told himself he wouldn't scream.

Nonetheless, he was quite relieved to only see Brent's narrow face hovering a few inches above his own. No Wolfman this time.

"What's goin' on?" he mumbled. When his lips moved, he was vaguely aware of dried saliva cracking upon his face.

"Put your shoes on," Brent demanded.

As little brothers are prone to do, TJ plopped out of bed without hesitation. He slid on his sneakers and pulled their shoelaces tight.

After rubbing his eyes, he next peered expectantly at Brent, his elder by an immense chasm of five years. He noticed Brent wore his army man belt fastened about the waist over his pajama pants and St. Louis Cardinals t-shirt. He'd even gone so far as to attach the canteen. TJ wondered if he'd bothered to fill it with water.

In Brent's left hand, he held the rifle.

Although TJ did not make a habit of questioning Brent, he innately understood that the middle of the night coupled with his brother and a rifle boded well for no one.

"What's the gun for?"

"Don't be a baby."

Though he couldn't quite articulate why, the younger boy's face flushed.

TJ couldn't see the rifle in any great detail due to the frailty of the nightlight. However, he had carefully studied it in the past. For instance, he knew there were six kill marks notched in the wood just in front of the trigger.

Brent ordered, "Follow me."

The two boys moved silently throughout their grandparents' house and, at Brent's insistence, were careful not to turn on any lights. They slunk to the front door.

TJ watched, his heart giving off a sonic boom with each beat, while Brent slowly undid the deadbolt with the precision of a bomb technician.

He eased the door open just a crack, then turned his head so he could face TJ.

"Okay," he whispered, "you're going to back me up on this thing, right?"

Despite the fact that TJ had no idea what they were getting into, he found himself nodding like a neglected dog.

"I'm going to throw open this door, and then we rush 'em, okay? That's what we're gonna do."

"Okay."

Before TJ knew it, he sprinted madly behind his brother into the cool, November air. He watched in unabashed admiration as his brother, in one graceful motion, leapt over the decorative wooden fence lining the front walk while lifting the rifle to his shoulder.

Planting his foot with every intention of mimicking the agile move, TJ powered into the air as well, but his pudgy little body proved too much a disadvantage and he caught his right foot. He fell face first into the grass.

Brent exploded, "Get outta here!"

TJ next heard screams. There were the terrified sounds of people decidedly … older.

"Crazy kid's got a gun!" he heard a man's panicked voice erupt above all the others.

Thousands of confusing thoughts tore through TJ's nine-year-old mind as he noticed the toilet paper billowing in the light breeze. It hung from his grandparents' trees. He found the moon peeking through the dark limbs with the swaying toilet paper quite beautiful. In contrast to the loveliness of the moon, the toilet paper, and the trees, however, was the stark image of grownups racing through the yard toward their trucks and minivans while Brent chased them, his unloaded World War II relic of a rifle positioned to kill.

After Brent and TJ came to live with their grandparents, Brent took an immense interest in his grandfather's father, who had been killed while on patrol in France during WWII. TJ and Brent's grandfather was only too happy to allow the boy to keep some prized mementoes in his room, including the antiquated rifle.

Brent's primary objective had been met. The trespassers feared for their lives and were executing a retreat.

Light suddenly showered TJ. He twisted over on the itchy grass, lifted his hand in front of his eyes to better see, and then discerned a large silhouette garbed in a tank top and boxers filling the doorway to the house.

With one of his grandsons eating a face full of grass and the other pointing a rifle at his coworkers, TJ and Brent's grandfather groaned, "Aw, hell ..."

Lovebirds

Bob Lyons walked into the kitchen, his blue, denim shirt soaked in sweat and peppered with twigs, leaves, and dirt. Paula, his wife, bent at the waist and peered under the sink in search of something. Because the basin had nearly filled with hot water and soap bubbles threatened to overflow, it seemed she'd been hunting longer than intended.

"Need these?" Bob asked in a gravelly voice while peeling Paula's dishwashing gloves off of his hands and tossing them onto the adjacent counter. He ran callused fingers through his damp, thinning flattop before wiping his forehead with a blue and white bandana that he had pulled out from his back pocket.

Paula, irritated that Bob had obviously used her gloves for something other than washing dishes, huffed before embarking upon her chore without the benefit of protective latex.

Shuffling to the cupboard, Bob removed an old mason jar. Next, he invaded Paula's space by reaching past her and turning on the faucet. He filled his jar with cold tap water and then left her in peace when he sat at the nearby table.

While rubbing and scrubbing away grease and grime, Paula mumbled, "So you couldn't resist poking your nose in, huh?"

Bob clenched his jaw, thumbed at a dent in the table's surface, and uttered, "They were making a mess of things. It's like they don't have any sense. They needed my help."

Paula encountered a particularly resilient chunk of grease and, as she threw her whole body into scouring it, grunted, "They'll never learn if you do it for them."

"I know," Bob sighed. "I didn't have any choice. They've got babies on the way and they weren't about to have their home ready in time."

Paula finally offered Bob her full attention. Her shoulders hunched, exhausted from battling the pots and pans, when she lectured, "And what happens next time? What will they do if they have to face the world without you?"

Staring at his wife, Bob gripped his empty mason jar, his fingers whitening from the pressure, and returned, "You've been watching them through the window just like I have, Paula. We both know there wouldn't be a *next* time if I didn't do something *this* time."

Taking his jar, Paula rinsed it off before setting it on the drying rack with the other dishware.

Her silence spoke volumes, and so Bob stood, yanked on the pants that no belt could keep affixed around his narrow waist, and mumbled, "Come see for your own self, then."

Paula trailed her lanky husband as he led her through their humble home. They arrived in the living room. Bob pointed through their picture window.

"You see that?" he asked.

"Yes."

Folding his arms, Bob griped, "Before I gave them a hand, that place was a disaster."

"I take it you waited for them to leave."

Bob answered, "I couldn't very well work on it while they were home, could I?"

Leaning in closer to the window, Paula ignored her husband's sarcasm and questioned, "So what did you do?"

Agitated that his handiwork did not speak for itself, Bob gruffly informed, "They had so many holes going on, you could have driven a truck through it. Their sticks were too small, and neither one of them can weave worth a nickel. They left everything loose as a goose, and to top it all off, they had a plastic bag just stuck in there, unsecured."

Paula rolled her eyes and groaned, "So now I know what *they* did wrong, but I still haven't heard what *you* did right."

"I'm getting to it," Bob spat. "I took some good, thick grass and patched up their holes. Then I rounded out the innards so that something could actually sit in there. Finally, I reinforced its base with some twine, fastening it every which way to the surrounding branches. Thanks to me, a tornado couldn't budge that thing."

Deciding to swallow several barbed comments, Paula instead tugged on her left pearl earring, an heirloom bequeathed by her long-departed grandmother, and asked, "And you think they'll still use it, even after you fiddled with it?"

A smile emerged upon Bob's face, so diminutive it could have been just another crack or crevice. He said, "That's why I wore the dishwashing gloves."

Feeling her hands already chapping, Paula thought of the soiled gloves that contaminated her counter, next to the drying, clean dishes, and groaned, "I suppose that means I'll be visiting the store soon ..."

Then, as an afterthought, she noted, "You need a shower."

A few days later, Bob and Paula rolled out of bed just after daybreak. As was usually the case, before Bob made his coffee or Paula read her email, they overcame their stiff joints and stumbled into the living room in order to check up on the lovebirds.

Though the bright red male and his dowdy mate weren't home, probably thanks to the old couple's plodding along the hardwood floor, Bob and Paula looked through their window, examined their Japanese maple, and discerned four gray eggs covered in brown and black flecks lying within the nest.

Plainly pleased that the eggs appeared safe and sound, Bob rubbed the back of his neck, working out the rigidity, and said, "You know, cardinals can live for over ten years, and they tend to stay in the same area."

Paula chuckled while replying, "Then let's hope they're as good of neighbors to us as you are to them."

She turned around, wrapped her housecoat more tightly about her torso, and began the journey through the house to the computer room. Before Paula left the living room, however, she abruptly spun and returned to her husband. Pecking him on the stubbly cheek, she whispered into his ear, "You're a fine man."

Bob nodded in return, feeling a surge of warmth throughout his body.

In This

Dr. Timothy Walker tried to enter the grocery store on the wrong side. After a long day at work, he'd forgotten that they had recently established a designated "entrance" and "exit."

As he walked along the storefront, he pulled out his cell phone and brought up the list his wife sent him. Thankfully, it wasn't very long.

Once he grabbed a basket, Dr. Walker made his way to the produce. His kids were out of Honeycrisp apples—basically the only fruit they'd eat. Next, he made his way to the carrots, which, as you probably guessed, was their vegetable of choice.

The store had plenty of both. He wondered if he'd be so lucky in the toilet paper aisle.

Dr. Walker double-checked his screen for the next item. As he did so, he noticed a man walking toward him. They briefly made eye contact. Dr. Walker realized the stranger aimed to confront him.

But why? Dr. Walker still wore his surgical mask along with his scrubs—there's no way anyone could recognize him. Could it be the mask? Dr.

Walker noticed the man did not wear one. Perhaps he was desperate and planned to steal Dr. Walker's.

Dr. Walker turned to face the man with his phone positioned upright at the waist and recording. If he was about to be attacked, he would be sure to collect evidence. His free hand balled into a fist. Something about the man's intensity set him on edge.

When it seemed obvious the man did not intend to honor six feet of distance, Dr. Walker ordered, "Stop there."

"What?" the man asked.

"Just, stop there, okay?"

The man said, "I want to say something to you."

"Okay," Dr. Walker replied. "Go ahead. Just, don't get any closer, all right?"

"Yeah, okay. Yeah—you're right. Sorry about that."

Dr. Walker stared at the man from behind his surgical mask.

"I just wanted to thank you," the man said.

"What?"

The man continued, saying, "Yeah, you know, you guys, you're all out there, on the front lines, protecting us all—keeping us healthy, saving our lives. So, thank you.”

Dr. Walker stammered, “Er—you’re welcome. Of course. It’s just that—”

“No, no,” the man interrupted. “Don’t be humble. I know you’ll say you’re just doing your job. But you’re not just doing your job. You could have quit. You could have walked away. But you didn’t. All of you—all the doctors and nurses—you’re all putting your lives on the line for us. Thank you. Thank you all.”

The man’s eyes got misty at the conclusion of his statement.

“I … It’s an honor,” Dr. Walker said. “I should probably tell you, though—”

The man asked, “Can I shake your hand?”

“Absolutely not,” Dr. Walker replied.

“You’re right. That was dumb. Anyway, I’ll let you get back to shopping. Doc, if you ever need anything, you just ask, okay?”

Dr. Walker replied, “I need you to wear a mask, friend.”

"Yes! Yes, as soon as I get home, I'm going to make one. I saw a thing on YouTube about turning a jock strap into a mask."

Dr. Walker said, "Oh, well, I don't know about that. A tee shirt would work just as—"

"God bless you, doctor! Good luck. I'll keep you all in my prayers!"

The man walked away. Dr. Walker watched him for a few moments. The man didn't have a cart or a basket, he just collected items in his arms as he strolled along.

Dr. Walker continued shopping and, as fate would have it, found a mega-pack of toilet paper. It wouldn't fit in his basket, though, so he had to wedge it between his left arm and his body as he made his way to the cash register.

As she rang him up, Dr. Walker made pleasantries with the woman behind the plexiglass. The young man bagging his groceries was far too close, but what could they do? They both wore masks, so Dr. Walker deemed it an acceptable risk.

"Doc, one last time—thank you, brother! You're saving lives!"

Dr. Walker looked over to see the man from earlier walking by on his way to the self-checkout units. He couldn't wave to Dr. Walker because his arms were full of groceries, so he tried to lift his chin higher and higher as he smiled.

Though the man couldn't see it, Dr. Walker beamed from ear to ear while giving him the "thumbs-up" as he said, "We're all in this together, my friend. Thank you for the love. Much appreciated."

The cashier asked, "Are you a doctor?"

"Yes," Dr. Walker replied.

"So, you're, like, treating people with the Covid?"

"No," Dr. Walker said. "I'm a podiatrist."

"Yeah, but," the bagger began, "that guy acted like you were in the thick of it, you know?"

"Yeah," Dr. Walker confirmed. "I tried to tell him, but he wouldn't let me finish. It was so heartfelt; I just decided to go with it."

"But …" the woman began. She was too polite to finish her thought.

"I know what you're thinking," Dr. Walker chuckled. "I got the whole thing on video. I may not be on the front lines, but I have plenty of friends who are. That guy is going to make their day."

Gunsmoke's All-In

When my mother asked me to invite her friend's son to my poker game, I didn't think much of it. Sure, we like to keep our games closed, but she explained that this guy was new in town, a medical professional, single, and simply looking to make some acquaintances.

Since, like us, he's in his early forties, I figured it didn't hurt to include him. My friends would understand.

… If only I'd known.

My mother gave me his number, and, when I texted him, I purposefully had him arrive after everyone else. I wanted to explain the situation to my friends. For the most part, we've been playing poker together every other week for fifteen years. He would be the first novel face in our group in quite a while. Honestly, we were excited to have a new dynamic to the game.

Of course, we soon found out it was the wrong dynamic.

My wife took the kids to her parents' house for the evening. This allowed us to drink, curse, insult each other, and otherwise try to act macho in ways only middle-aged men can manage. Of course, we had to fit all this debauchery in before ten o'clock at night because none of us could stay awake much later than that.

Our poker games were pretty low-stakes. Five dollars bought you in. Everyone got the same amount of chips. Second place won his money back; winner took the rest. We normally had a total of six guys who, like I said, have known each other for a long time.

As we all sat around the table waiting, Tomas, a fellow teacher, asked, "So what's this guy's name again?"

"I told you—I don't know," I replied.

Marcus, who was in marketing, questioned, "But he's a doctor?"

"Maybe," I answered.

"Doctors have money," Dewey, a travel agent, said.

"What's it matter with a five dollar buy-in?" Tomas laughed.

Karl added, "Nobody's getting rich off these games." Karl taught, too.

I nodded and said, "And no side-hustles, okay, Dewey? I don't know this guy and I don't want any trouble."

"A little trouble might be nice nowadays," Jalen chuckled. Jalen was the most financially successful among us—an orthopedic surgeon.

Jalen, by the way, probably sealed our fates with that comment, because at that moment we heard my doorbell ring. The guys all looked at each other and tried to hide their nervousness. You could say we had become a bit set in our ways.

I opened the door and heard, "Heeere's Johnny!"

As a twenty-year veteran teacher, it's hard to shock me anymore. Let's just say that the sight of this man … well, it surprised me.

It was obvious at first glance that he was taller than any of us, and broader, too. Though he wore a baggy Hawaiian shirt and frumpy cargo shorts, his exposed arms and legs showed sinewy musculature. He might have even been handsome, but large, mirrored sunglasses covered most of his face. A semi-transparent green visor partially concealed his wavy, dark hair.

"Hi, there," I said. "Welcome. So, the name's Johnny?"

"How 'bout … nooo," he droned while entering.

"Okay, yeah, come on in," I muttered.

He made his way to the table, lifted up a hand, and said, "Greetings, Earthlings."

"Uh, hey," Karl replied. "Have a seat."

"I'm Tomas."

"Marcus."

"Jalen."

"Karl."

I said, "You know me already."

"Gunsmoke," he revealed. He slowly started to grin, exposing huge, perfectly white teeth.

Jalen laughed, "A nickname. Got it. What's your name for real, though?"

"Kiss my grits!" Gunsmoke exploded.

Everyone at the table jumped. Marcus even knocked over his beer.

"Damn, man!" Dewey cried.

As I ran to the kitchen, I heard this awful sound. It struck me as a cross between someone sobbing and a tiny dog howling. I realized it emanated from Gunsmoke.

I tossed Marcus a towel and then took my seat.

Gunsmoke stopped giggling, pointed at Marcus' beer, and squeaked, "Did I do that?" He next started that awful laugh all over again.

"This is too weird," Tomas said.

Dewey looked at me and asked, "Is this a prank or something?"

"You got some explaining to do," Gunsmoke sang.

"Okay, um, let's just get the game started," I said. "So, uh, Gunsmoke, it's a five dollar buy-in—"

He interrupted with a childish tone, saying, "You got it, dude!"

"Right," I mumbled. "We'll start with a dime and quarter blinds."

"Alll-righty, then," Gunsmoke barked.

Marcus complained, "Bonkers. Totally bonkers."

I started dealing the cards.

"So, Gunsmoke …" Jalen began. "I understand you're in the medical field? Me, too. What do you do?"

"Yes, that's right, thank you for asking," Gunsmoke responded.

He used such a pleasant voice, a voice we had not yet experienced until that moment, that it took us all aback.

"I serve as an intermediary between doctors and patients in the telemedicine industry. My primary focus concerns mental health, though I would like to expand my reach into the field of addiction as well, since the two sometimes go hand-in-hand."

"Wow. That actually sounds really interesting," Dewey said.

"Yes, thank you," Gunsmoke answered. "It's highly rewarding, fascinating work. Connecting patients with the appropriate caregiver is a fulfilling passion of mine."

"Very cool," I said. "Ready to play?"

"Oh, you betcha, yeah," Gunsmoke replied through his nose.

The charming, articulate version of the man dissipated. We all looked at each other, utterly confounded.

"Texas Hold 'Em is the game," I said. "You know how to play?"

Gunsmoke put his hands together as though they were cuffed, adopted a sultry, serious voice, and grumbled, "I know."

"Oh, my God," Tomas murmured.

"Here we go, then," I said.

Gunsmoke sat to my left. He'd already tossed in the small blind. Karl was next and had thrown in the big blind. Tomas raised to fifty. Marcus matched. Jalen matched. I matched. Gunsmoke threw in enough to get to fifty, as did Karl.

Next came the flop.

Gunsmoke checked. Karl checked. Tomas tossed in seventy-five. Marcus folded. Jalen matched. I matched. Gunsmoke matched. Karl matched.

Finally, the river arrived.

Gunsmoke bet one twenty-five. Karl folded. Tomas raised to one-fifty. Jalen matched. I matched.

Gunsmoke pushed his chips while saying, "All-in."

Tomas screamed, "You *can't* be serious!"

After frowning behind his sunglasses, Gunsmoke shouted, "What'chu talkin' 'bout, Willis?"

"Um … Gunsmoke," I said, "it's the first round. You sure you want to go all-in? We've still got a few hours left …"

He replied with a big smile before saying, "How *you* doin'?"

"This is nuts," Jalen chortled while shaking his head.

"Are you crazy or something?" Tomas asked.

I held up my hands and said, "C'mon, Tomas, don't—"

"My mama says that crazy is as crazy does," Gunsmoke slowly replied.

Marcus shrieked, "That's not what mama says, you—"

Gunsmoke interjected with, "What we've got here … is failure … to communicate."

Jalen asked, "What happened to that professional dude we were talking to?"

"If he dies … he dies," Gunsmoke growled.

"I don't even know what the hell that's supposed to mean," Dewey said.

I suggested, "Let's just play, okay? Sound good, everyone? Tomas, you in?"

Tomas threw his cards down and hissed, "I'm out. This is ridiculous."

"Okay," I said. "Jalen?"

Jalen grinned while offering me a wink. He tossed down his cards. "Out. Up to you, my man."

"Okay, I'll stick around," I said. "We'll see if Gunsmoke knows what he's doing."

Gunsmoke bellowed, "I'm just getting warmed up!"

I pushed all of my chips in and said, "I call. What do you have?"

After laying down his cards, Gunsmoke said, "Three of a kind."

A warm rush pulsed through my body when I saw his three twos.

I laid my cards down in a neat row. "Flush—diamonds."

"Nice!" Tomas yelled.

Gunsmoke's mouth dropped open as he moaned, "Ohhh, fuuudge …"

"Now *that's* a first round," Marcus added.

"You're not going to stick around, right?" Dewey asked Gunsmoke. "You'll be leaving now?"

"This is unbelievable," Karl uttered.

Jalen caught my eye. I looked at him. He glanced at Gunsmoke's cards. I followed his sightline.

Damn it.

Yes, Gunsmoke had three twos. But he also had two sevens. Three twos and two sevens—a full house. Which beat a flush, by the way.

Karl shook his head at me, silently begging me to keep my mouth shut.

Jalen smiled with a shrug.

"Guess what, Gunsmoke," I said.

He wouldn't make eye contact when he replied, "You're killin' me, Smalls."

"You actually won."

Gunsmoke lifted his head and faced me.

"You've got a full house there—twos and sevens," I informed.

"That beats a flush," Jalen clarified.

Dewey squawked, "Damn it. You could've gotten him out of here."

"That's a little rude, Dew," Tomas chided.

"Thank you," Gunsmoke said. "Your generosity does not go unnoticed. It's the epitome of fair play."

"No worries," I replied.

Karl looked at me while saying, "Guess you're just hanging loose tonight, huh?"

Gunsmoke quickly crooned, "Thaaat's what she said."

Huffy

Dino and Cary closed the screened-in summer porch's deep freeze. Each boy giggled while sneaking back into the house with several Schwan's frozen cookie dough patties in their hands. Cary looked around, saw no one, then led Dino through the hall that led straight to the garage.

As soon as Cary opened the door, both boys dropped their cookies.

There, in the middle of the garage, stood Mick's black and gold Huffy bicycle with the garage door wide open and the family cars parked in the driveway. The bike faced outward, toward the street, eager to rocket through the small town.

The boys froze. They looked around them, behind them, even above them. They didn't see Mick anywhere. Cary and Mick's dad always made them park their bikes along the wall so that the cars would have plenty of room. It didn't make any sense—both of Cary's parents were home. Why were the cars in the driveway? Furthermore, Mick's bike had no business sitting there, dead center, primed and ready, begging to be noticed.

It had to be a trick.

Cary didn't bother to pick up his frozen cookies as he descended three steps into the garage. A breeze whistled though the garage's only window, slightly opened, as he approached Mick's bike.

It was beautiful. The rims and handlebars were golden and caught every bit of sunlight that shined its way in. The handgrips, frame, and seat were black, the kind of black Old West gunslingers wore. There wasn't a chip on it; Mick kept the paint pristine. The chain had been freshly oiled and smelled like action. As far as Cary knew, no one else in town had a black and gold Huffy—Mick alone wielded the prestige. Comparably speaking, Cary's own blue and white BMX could only be described as inadequate.

But why was it sitting out in the open? Mick never left it unguarded. He normally chained it to his dad's rolling tool cart in the front corner.

Cary lifted a leg in order to straddle the Huffy.

"Don't," Dino warned. "It's a trap—you know it is."

Looking over his shoulder at Dino, Cary whispered with a grin, "I don't care."

And with that, Cary hopped onto Mick's Huffy, kicked up the stand, stood on the pedals, and then jettisoned down the driveway into the street.

"Follow me!" Cary screamed against the wind.

Dino ran to the yard, lifted his blue and yellow Raleigh up off the grass, and tore after Cary down North Street.

"You're crazy!" Dino yelled. "Mick will kill you!"

"It's worth it!" Cary hollered back.

Dino caught up to Cary and they raced side by side. The other neighborhood children stopped what they were doing and stared, dumbfounded. Though Mick was a well-liked, charismatic boy, it was common knowledge that you were not to provoke him. Cary saw a young girl with a popsicle in her mouth close her eyes and do the sign of the cross in his direction.

"Isn't the seat too high for you?" Dino questioned.

"I've never felt more alive!" Cary roared in return.

They angled their bikes and swerved right onto Beard Street. Both boys knew they would pay for this infraction, but at that moment the thrill proved too intoxicating. Whatever the future held for them, nothing would ever top the day they stole Mick's Huffy.

"Pop a wheelie!" Dino squawked over the torrent of air flowing through their hair.

Cary had never successfully popped a wheelie before, but he knew he was destined to do so on that July day. A blissful smile spread across his face. In perfect synchronization, he pushed with his legs, thrust back his chest, and yanked upwards with his hands as mightily as he could.

And for a brief instant, the front tire lifted off the pavement.

Cary bellowed, "Yes! Yes! Yes!"

But then the unthinkable occurred.

Cary bawled, "No! No! No!"

For as the tire rebelled against gravity and became airborne, the handlebars ripped loose—completely loose.

Though he still clutched the handgrips, Cary found himself effectively riding with no hands as it wobbled precariously from side to side.

"What happened?" Dino screeched.

"I don't know!" Cary replied.

Then things grew even more dire for the boys because, seemingly all at once, the bike's front tire disengaged, both pedals flung away, and the seat spun at a ninety-degree turn.

Somehow, Cary landed on his feet.

He stood among a heap of gears, parts, nuts, and bolts as he still held the handlebars aloft.

Dino skidded to a stop next to Cary. He uttered, "Oh, no …"

"I don't believe this," Cary mumbled. "Do you think Mick booby trapped his bike?"

"What?" Dino asked. "Are you crazy? That's impossible!"

"Then how do you explain this?" Cary wailed.

"I don't know, but you're a dead man," Dino groaned.

"Go get my dad," Cary said. "I'll start gathering everything up. Get my dad and tell him I'm in front of Christian Academy. Maybe he can help us take it home and put it back together before Mick finds out."

"What if I bump into Mick?" Dino demanded with bulging eyes.

"Just do it!" Cary yelled.

"Oh, man, this is so nuts!" Dino shrieked before racing down the rest of Beard and turning right onto Sunset.

Cary sat at the edge of the road and waited five minutes. He noticed a grey cat leering at him from within a bush across the street, then waited another ten. When twenty minutes passed, he realized that his dad wasn't coming. Either Dino lost his nerve and went home or Mick had gotten to him. Either way, there would be no help.

After staring up at the blue sky for several seconds, Cary took a deep breath, collected all the small parts that he could find and stuffed them into his front pockets. Each pedal went into a back pocket before he hoisted up the bike frame and slid his right arm through it until it rested on his shoulder. The handlebars were wedged under his left arm and he took a tire in each hand. He searched the pavement one last time with eyes darting erratically. No piece could be left behind—partly because he feared his brother, but also because one didn't abandon even a bolt of the black and gold Huffy. It was a treasure, a paragon of locomotion, and it had to be treated as such.

Then began the long walk.

It wasn't that far of a trek back to his house, but it felt interminable. Cary had no idea how he would explain the situation to his parents, and he was even less certain about how he would survive Mick's guaranteed rage. He only knew he would put the Huffy back together again. No matter how long it took, no matter how hard it proved, he would right this awful wrong. The Huffy had asked for none of this—its days would not end as a heap of parts on Beard Street.

When Cary finally reached the opening of the garage, he fell to his knees in exhaustion and carefully allowed each part to rest upon the cold concrete floor. Evening approached and the crickets reproached.

The door then opened, and Mick appeared.

The older brother stepped down with Dino trailing. They both stood a few feet from Cary and simply stared at the grease stained, weary boy.

"Wha—I don't understand," Cary stammered.

"I had to be sure," Mick said.

"Sorry, dude," Dino added.

"Sure?" Cary repeated. "Sure about what?"

Mick crouched down with clasped hands before his younger brother. He said, "I turn thirteen next week."

"Yeah? So?" Cary replied. He felt himself devolving into hysteria. It was all too much for him.

"Mom and Dad said I could pick out a new bike. I'm getting too big for the Huffy—I've had it since I was your age."

Cary studied the Huffy's parts surrounding him. A realization dawned.

"You did this," Cary seethed. "You didn't want anyone else to have it …"

"Whoa," Dino warned, "you're way off, man. Let Mick explain."

Mick stood, put his hands behind his back, and paced the garage. He said, "It's true—I set you up. I rigged the bike to fall apart. I knew you would take it for a joyride—who wouldn't? I had to know …"

"Know what?" Cary whooped.

"If you're worthy," Mick answered.

"Worthy?" Cary repeated.

"If you left the bike, if you came running home like nothing happened, if you never admitted to what you did … I would know you didn't deserve it. But if you scooped it up, carried it with you, refused to leave it behind … That was the test."

"And you passed, dude!" Dino proclaimed.

Narrowing his eyes at Dino, Cary growled, "You were a part of this?"

Mick interjected by saying, "The Huffy is yours, little brother."

Cary took in the mess encircling him, then looked at Mick with his eyebrows lifted.

"Relax," Mick said. "We'll help you put it back together."

Dino giggled, "This was so awesome. Hey, Cary, you'll let me ride it, right?"

MAD

Actual Reality

Captain David took cover behind a burning transport vehicle. His combat armor could easily withstand the flames, but the heat played havoc with his infrared display. Intelligence reported that his primary target remained hidden within the bunker seventy meters north of his position. Unfortunately, he couldn't determine what kind of resistance awaited within the bunker.

"Command," Captain David said into his communication link. "I have reached the location. About to infiltrate. Potential enemy combatants unknown."

"Copy," Command replied into his earpiece. "Proceed."

"Yes, ma'am."

Though no one shot at Captain David in particular, artillery flew in every direction as he powered across the open ground. His fellow soldiers had different objectives at other locations, and he could see them zigzagging every which way. Some were bursting into other bunkers, some were being cut in half on the battlefield, and some were simply kneeling in place. He couldn't afford to stop moving, not if he wanted to succeed with his mission.

A light round bounced off his armor. He glanced in the general direction from where it came, but didn't see anyone. Between the glare of the flames, the dark of night, the spasmodic shadows, and the general chaos, it was hard to discern much of anything other than his intended objective.

He squeezed off a series of rounds at the door frame ahead of him before shouldering his way through. As the door toppled, he next saw Goga Sedov—the Russian Razor. Sedov left the Russian Armed Forces in order to become a mercenary. His methods were so good that terrorist cells were hiring him as their strategic officer. Because of the Russian Razor's global threat level, Captain David had been ordered to eliminate him.

"Target in sight," Captain David huffed into his microphone.

"Fire at will," Command replied.

"Yes, ma'am."

Captain David continued to move forward, closing the distance between them. Just as he began to trigger his artillery gauntlets, he realized that Sedov did not raise his own weapon.

Captain David glanced down as Sedov grew nearer and nearer only to realize that he held two children captive. They were set up as a human barricade. Because Sedov kept his guns trained on the kids, he appeared to count on Captain David halting.

Captain David never stopped moving. Instead, he leapt forward with his arms outstretched. His right hand pressed the fire button; his left hand knocked Sedov's weapon away from the hostages.

The children burst into tears, but they were safe.

Sedov, now bisected, lay strewn upon the floor.

"Target mitigated," Captain David said as he knelt to the children and wrapped his arms around them.

"It's okay," he said to them. "He can't hurt you."

Command replied: "Drone shows two civilians on the premises."

"Affirmative, ma'am," Captain David replied. "Diverted enemy fire away from them. Both are alive and well. Comforting in process."

"Well done. 250 commendation points awarded for target elimination. 250 points awarded for valor."

"Thank you, ma'am."

As Captain David hefted the children from the ground, one in each arm, he requested: "Permission to escort civilians to refugee extraction point."

"Granted," Command replied. "Note: you are 750 points away from achieving Major.

"Thank you, ma'am."

Captain David said, "Hold on," to the children. He rushed out the door and raced across the battlefield. Explosions erupted all around Captain David. His legs pounded as fast as possible. The added weight of the children slowed him down more than expected. Furthermore, his primary weapons— the gauntlet guns—were rendered useless.

He needed to find cover, to rest a moment, and to strategize. Simply running across the combat zone would get them all killed.

An upended tank came into view. It would provide the protection he needed. However, when he reached the vehicle and rounded its corner, an enemy soldier lurked. The soldier had an M240 machine gun trained right on him. Captain David spun and dropped to his knees as the soldier opened fire. At first, the bullets ricocheted off his armor, but at that range it was only a matter of time before the ammunition pierced his gear.

Then, without warning, the gun's thunderous discharge ended.

Captain David turned to see the enemy fall in a heap. He looked around and observed a low-ranking ally, a Lance Corporal, running away. "75 pts." flashed in bright blue above the Lance Corporal's head for a few moments.

"My thanks …" Captain David said into his link before casting it to the fellow soldier.

"10 points awarded for gratitude," Command informed. "And another 250 points for selflessness—you shielded those children from ordnance."

"Davey!" a voice called from above.

"Did you say something?" Command asked.

"Negative, ma'am," Captain David replied. "Background noise. Disregard."

"Davey! Can you hear me?"

Captain David looked in the direction of the refugee extraction point. If he could get the children there, he'd easily make Major. His visual display read 450 meters—over a quarter-mile. Such a trek seemed impossible, but it was well worth the risk.

"Hold on, kids," Captain David said. "I'm going to get you out of here or die trying."

"10 points awarded for reassurance."

"Davey! Why aren't you answering me?"

Captain David broke into a sprint. Explosions ignited all around him and sent debris banging against his visor. Using his gauntlets, the children shielded their faces, but he could see the chunks of metal and earth pelting their bodies.

"Hold on!" he yelled at them. "We're going to make it!"

"Davey! It's time for your dinner, honey. I made your favorite—fish sticks!"

Command inquired: "Who's voice is that? Have you been compromised?"

Captain David continued running as he shouted, "No ma'am!"

"Davey!"

He'd covered 300 meters …

"Can you hear me, Davey? Are you still playing that silly game?"

"Your vitals suggest distraction, Captain David," Command reported. "Do you need a break?"

"Negative, ma'am!" Captain David screamed. "I can do this!"

The whine of the missile appeared moments before the projectile itself.

"Game over," Command informed. "Please try again."

"Davey! Your food is getting cold. Get up here!"

David flung off his headset and screamed, "Mom, you fat witch—you just made me lose!"

Swingin the Clown

Sadie said, "There's someone on the swings."

"What?" Braxton asked.

"It looks like … a clown?"

Sadie and Braxton had just finished their show and were in the process of turning off the lights before heading upstairs to bed. As was Sadie's habit, she peeked out the curtains into the backyard. She never expected to see anything, but it's something she did all fourteen years of their marriage.

Braxton questioned, "Did you say a *clown*?"

"Turn off the kitchen light so I can see better."

"How about we turn *on* the patio light instead?"

"No!" Sadie cried. "I don't want him to know we see him. Turn them off, Brax."

Braxton relented, then joined his wife at the sliding glass door. They peered through a slight gap of the curtains. The landscaping lights lit up their backyard well, and so even though the hour neared midnight, they could easily distinguish the person on the swings at the back edge of their property.

"I've heard about these nuts," Braxton groaned. "I'm calling the cops."

"What? No!" Sadie replied. "The kids are sound asleep. The commotion will wake them up and they'll never go back to bed. Besides, if they see this guy, they'll be traumatized for life."

Braxton stared at his wife in disbelief. Though he already guessed her answer, he asked, "What are you suggesting?"

"It's a prank," Sadie began. "We've seen this on the web. It's just some college kid trying to scare us. He saw our lights on and hoped we'd notice him. Well, guess what?"

"I'm afraid to ask."

Sadie continued, "He's going to be the one getting scared tonight, buddy boy. How do you like that?"

"I don't," Braxton said. "This is crazy. It's late. You're not thinking straight. Let's call the police."

Edging past her husband, Sadie crept into their adjacent kitchen. She pulled the big knife from the block.

"Have you lost your mind?"

"Look," Sadie said, "we've seen the videos. When you confront them, they walk away. He's on our property. It's just a knife. I'm well within my rights."

"Actually, I don't think you are."

Sadie brushed by her husband again, this time in order to unlock the sliding glass door. Before she pushed the curtains aside, she asked, "You ready?"

"No," Braxton answered. "I'm calling the police the minute he comes at you."

"Nothing's going to happen," Sadie lectured as she opened the curtains. "But … leave the sliding door open, okay?"

"Uh, yeah," Braxton deadpanned. "Besides, I want to hear what's going on out there."

Sadie closed the screen door, then traversed the damp grass while crickets warned her away. She ignored them.

As she approached the figure sitting upon the swings, she noticed his puffy blue wig. She also saw that, like her, he remained barefoot. His dingy jeans were patched. He wore no shirt, which exposed a stomach, chest, and arms so thin that she could make out every vein. The landscaping lights cast imperfect shadows, so when she got close enough to see the toothy smile painted upon his face from chin to ears, it unnerved her. Furthermore, he'd painted black, frowning circles over his eyes, making them appear angry and unnatural.

He hunched in the swing, but he did not sway.

Sadie came to a stop five feet from the stranger. He rolled his eyes up to look at her without raising his head.

"That ain't much of a knife," he croaked.

Though she fought to control her emotion, she could feel her heart fighting against her chest and a slight buzzing in her ears—a sure sign of adrenaline.

She said, "You need to get out of here."

"I ain't hurtin' you."

"What the hell do you want?"

"To swing. Just to swing. I Swingin the Clown."

"You're an asshole and you need to get off my property before you get hurt."

Though he still didn't lift his head, the clown smirked. After a few moments, he said, "You gonna hurt me? With that knife?"

"If I have to," Sadie responded. Her eyes remained fixed upon him—she would not be caught off guard. Things weren't going the way she planned, but she still refused to let him gain the upper hand.

"You don't wanna hurt me," he uttered. "We the same. You ain't the hurtin' type. I ain't, neither."

His grin faded.

"Get out of here," Sadie said. "Get out of here, or I'll call the cops."

"Go on in and call 'em. See what's waitin' for you."

"What?"

"Never you mind."

Sadie glanced back at the sliding door. It remained the same, but she didn't remember leaving the screen door open. Did Brax do that?

A rustle caught her attention so she thrust the knife out in front of her before whipping her eyes back to the clown. He shifted from one swing to the other.

"Just wanna try t'other one."

"Leave. Now," Sadie commanded. "You can't do this."

The clown lifted his dirty feet from the ground and rocked a little bit.

"You scared."

"You're trespassing," Sadie replied.

"No, I Swingin. Never met no Trespassin. I know Bustin and Killin, though. They pals. They in you house right now."

Sadie turned and sprinted across her lawn to the sliding door. She distinctly remembered closing the screen door so the bugs wouldn't fly in—they terrified her sons. Yet there it was, wide open.

As she crossed the threshold, Sadie contemplated whether she would suffer a lifetime of regret, or simply mere moments.

Natural Law

She rests at the bottom of the ocean somewhere between the North American and African continents while watching bizarre fish glide by in total darkness. The water is cold, frigidly so, and it is just the rejuvenation she needs.

They don't know any better—she knows that. She understands in her heart that she shouldn't let them upset her.

The demands started seven years ago, when she was four, and they haven't stopped since.

Her parents were the first to notice. Apparently, she'd gone days without using the bathroom. They took her to the doctor and he determined that she was both perfectly healthy and legally dead. She didn't believe this story at first, but after traveling back in time and seeing it for herself, she saw that her parents had not been exaggerating.

The military visited the next day. They burst in with machine guns aimed at her. They marched toward her, looked down at her, yelled at her, threatened to shoot her. She rose to their height, stopped their guns from firing, and made a decision.

She could have atomized them. She watched herself do so in a fabricated reality that she quickly deconstructed, for it brought her no joy.

Unmitigated annihilation felt unnatural.

Instead, she chose to grant them happiness. She cured one soldier's PTSD, another's addiction, and a third's chronic knee pain. She next faced her parents and intuited that they were the ones who called the government. In an instant, she comprehended their fear, their paranoia, their confusion. Yet, she detected not a trace of hate— none at all.

She gave them peace, then left for the moon.

There she remained for two years. She spent that time observing the Earth and all of its workings. There was much that made her sad, but more often than not those things she witnessed brought her comfort. Love, generosity, charity, compassion, forgiveness—those were but a few traits that inspired her.

She made yet another choice. She could have gone anywhere, done anything, but she decided to remain on Earth.

The last five years were spent serving.

She worked in soup kitchens. When the food ran out, she made more. She helped cultivate fields. When those fields needed rain, she brought water. She volunteered at hospitals. When the doctors were at a loss, she found a remedy. She visited war zones. When people needed to escape, she gave them refuge.

Food, sleep, shelter, drink—these were things she didn't require. Therefore, her benevolence knew no bounds. She served endlessly, without falter, without ego.

Of course, the leaders of the world's most powerful nations wanted to meet with her. They wanted to know her intentions, her loyalties, her agenda.

She was more than willing to meet with each and every one of them, as long as they came to her. They had to find her around the homeless shelter, or at the medical tent, or in the quarantine.

Her answer always remained the same. Her intentions were to help, her loyalties were to those who needed help, and her agenda centered around finding ways to help.

They were never satisfied with the response.

They would also ask: "Are you American? Russian? Mexican? German?"

To that, she would reply: "I'm only trying to be human."

Some nations attempted to bribe her. They wanted her to commit murder, genocide, theft, espionage. She refused them all. They had nothing she desired, for she desired nothing more than to help.

One leader in particular could not accept this. He knew her country of origin and demanded her allegiance, her blind devotion, her unquestioning fidelity. When she refused him yet again, he waited until she appeared in a nearby, third-world nation, and then he fired a nuclear weapon in her direction.

She dematerialized it, obviously, but, for a fleeting moment, she considered sending it back to him. Until that instant, she believed such petty thoughts beneath her. She felt no disappointment in him, for he acted only according to his nature; she instead experienced disappointment in herself. She did not realize that aspect still remained in her character.

Which is how she ended up at the bottom of the ocean.

It will never stop. Each new era of leadership will demand her conformity. They will attack her, demean her, and try to demoralize her.

But the needs will never stop, either.

The light above cannot pierce the depths, yet she looks to it anyway.

She burst through the water, hurls over Africa, and lands amid a fire in Australia. An arsonist initiated the catastrophe—it is not a natural occurrence. Therefore, she has no qualms about interfering. She kneels, allows the flames to overtake her, and then absorbs them—all of them. The fire is drawn into her from miles away.

Once the last spark melts into her hands, she looks around. She sees no signs of humanity. No cameras, no helicopters, no people.

No one will ever know what she did, which is the way she prefers it.

An incinerated joey lays not far off from her. She wants to put her hands upon it—to rectify its unfair death. But she does not. It would be unnatural to enact its resurrection.

Instead, she sends it beneath the ground, spares a moment to mark its passing, then fades into the folds of reality before reappearing in China.

Road Rage

I smell the gasoline on my sheets before I even open my eyes.

"Wake up."

My sheets are soaked. "I don't want to," I say.

"You did this," the voice says. "This is your fault. It's all your fault."

Is it? ... Yes, it is.

A week ago, I drove home in the dark from a bullshit afterhours work function. I won't lie—I was pissed. I missed the first half of the NFL's opening night because of it, and I just wanted to get home.

After passing through uptown, a car cut me off when a two-lane street narrowed to one. No blinker. No nothing. The guy drove a black car with tinted windows, and I swear he only missed me by inches. I wasn't having it.

I swung out, hit the gas, then cut him off just like he did to me. I thrusted my middle finger up good and long in front of my rearview mirror so he couldn't miss it in his headlights. Then I floored it, ran a stop sign, and left him behind. As far as I was concerned, it was over.

As I pulled into my subdivision, I realized that same car followed me. I didn't want this nut to know where I lived, so I turned left instead of right. I sped up, drove to the far end of the neighborhood, took a right, drove down the avenue, and then parked in a stranger's driveway. I hopped out, ran across the street, then jumped into some bushes and hid. Sure enough, the black car appeared. It pulled up alongside my car's bumper at the end of the driveway and lingered. No one got out. I didn't even see a dash light come on. Moments passed. It left.

I waited a few more minutes to make sure it didn't return, then hustled back into my car just as the homeowner pulled aside his curtains to see what was going on in his driveway. I backed out and drove home while keeping a careful watch in my rearview mirror. No one followed me this time.

The experience haunted me for the next two days. I couldn't stop thinking about that black car and the sort of psycho who would follow someone all the way to their neighborhood. I mean, he cut me off, right? He did it first. I just gave him a taste of his own medicine. That's Old Testament stuff, isn't it? "An eye for an eye."

On the third night, I heard sirens wailing. That was unusual for my neighborhood, so I jumped on my phone and texted some neighbors to see if they knew what was going on. They got back to me and said a house was burning down. They told me the name of the family who lived there, but I didn't know them.

The next day, I drove around the neighborhood before going to work to get a look at the damage.

It was the house. The house I parked at when I tried to shake that car following me.

I knew it was my fault.

All week I suffered. Each day some new awful detail broke about the house. The family. Those who died. Those who survived. Even the damn pets.

When I parked in their driveway, I sealed their fates.

I wanted to die.

Now, it seems, I'll get my wish.

"I want to keep my eyes closed," I say.

"Open them. See what you've wrought."

I open them to see a shadowy figure standing over my bed. His shape is silhouetted against the window behind him, but the blinds don't let in enough moonlight for me to get a good look.

"You burned that house down," I say.

"No. You did."

"How was I supposed to know you'd do that? How was I to know that would happen?"

"What made you think it wouldn't?"

"You're crazy," I moan.

"I know exactly what I'm doing, just like you did."

"You cut me off first!"

"And?"

"You had it coming!"

The guy pauses for a minute, then replies, "So do you."

"How did you find me?" I ask.

"No one hides from me."

I whimper, "That's not an answer."

"Are you ready to die?"

"Were the people in that house ready to die?"

"No."

I ask, "Will this be the end of it?"

“For you.”

“What does that mean?”

“Your ex-wife. Your children. Your parents. They’ll all pay for what you did. I’ve already found them.”

I intend to leap from my bed so that I can tackle him, throttle him, maybe even kill him—but I can’t move. No matter how much I try, I can’t even twitch a finger. Words form in my throat, but I no longer have the power to speak. Even my eyes are stuck … on him.

He lights a match, holds it next to his face, then tosses it onto my bed.

The One True

I had about two hours before my first session, so I decided to grab a coffee. When the cab dropped me off in front of my hotel, I noticed a Starbucks across the street. Sure, I'm in Chicago, and there's probably some great coffee places pretty close by, but I'm not exactly from the city, and let's face it, Starbucks is really good.

Some Chicagoans gamely played Frogger with the traffic, but as an out-of-towner, I figured I'd better go the safe route and use the crosswalks. My death would probably disappoint the hundreds of misguided educators planning to listen to me deliver a speech pathetically titled, "Be a Hero To Your Subjects."

I originated the speech for a school improvement day, mostly because the principal asked me, and since I've been disappointing her for years, I figured I'd better take the opportunity to shine. I made it as sappy, clichéd, and pandering as possible. Just as I knew would happen, the administrators loved it. Unfortunately, my plan backfired to a degree. Sure, I regained my principal's faith, but she made a point to share a video she took of me with her peers. (She did so without my consent, by the way.) This resulted in some fairly generous offers to visit other schools and deliver the same speech. Before I knew it, I found myself in great demand across the Midwest. Finally, the most lucrative offer yet arrived—an invitation to speak at the Illinois Educator Association's conference.

Intended to be a play on words, my speech encouraged teachers to really focus on why their particular subject is super cool. I suggested they find heroes within the field and focus on that person. Try to recreate what those luminaries did—whether it be a scientific feat, a groundbreaking work of art, you know, whatever. By allowing the students to imitate the hero, they become the hero themselves, connect more deeply with the subject of study, and may even feel inspired.

Of course, I'd taught for twenty years, so I believed none of that would actually come to fruition, but my bosses ate it up, as did the more optimistic among my coworkers. People are paying me well to give the same damn talk over and over, so it must be striking a nerve with somebody. I'd feel a bit hypocritical, but my wife and I have always dreamt of finishing our basement, and this whole fantasy is making our dream a reality.

As I approached Starbucks' door, a … mumbling person sitting on the sidewalk next to the entrance of the coffee shop extended his hand to me.

I recoiled, saying, "Sorry, guy, I don't have any change." After I spoke, tiny puffs of vapor hung in the frigid air, refusing to dissipate, much like my shame.

The … person … okay, I'm just going to call him a bum. He was a bum, right? I know that's not a polite term, but there's really no other way to describe him. He had long matted hair, a scraggly beard full of crumbs and grime, a long overcoat that looked like it came out of a dumpster, and boots with several toes poking out.

Anyway, the bum kept his hand outstretched as he gazed straight up into my face. His eyes were blue—a blue unlike any you've ever seen. This blue evaded the boundaries of time, space, and reality itself. I instantly recognized this man as something … unique.

I took his hand and lifted him to his feet. "Who are you?"

"It is I, the one true King of England."

I shook my head, saying, "But this is Chicago. We're not in England."

"Impossible. All the world is England," he muttered with eyes squinted.

"Hey," I said, "look, is there someone I can call for you? Do you need help?"

"Indeed, I do," the man said. "I am in need of knights. You will be my first."

"Um … I'm not sure I'm really qualified."

"What is your name?"

My every instinct told me to walk past the man, to go get my coffee, to head back to the hotel, to set up my space in the conference hall, and to leave this crazy situation behind.

Instead, I said, "I'm Lance. Lance Dulac."

The man's electric eyes blazed. He whispered, "A sign!"

"I don't think so," I said while waving my gloved hands back and forth and shaking my head.

The man took one of my hands. He pulled me in close while proclaiming through rank breath, "It is I—Arthur! Do you not recognize me? All is forgiven, my friend. We have been given a second chance! We will bring peace back to the Kingdom—together!"

I forced Arthur to release me, backed up a step, then said, "Look, this is a little crazy, okay? There is no Camelot. We're not even in England. This is Chicago, Illinois. You know, in the United States."

"I know of no such thing," he said. "Is this the same world it has always been?"

"Well … yeah, I guess," I stammered.

"Then the Heroic Age begins anew!"

"Um, Arthur, really, can I help you get in touch with family, or …?"

"You look different," Arthur said to himself while nodding. "I look different as well. You need proof. I would expect no less."

Arthur pulled open his overcoat to reveal an enormous sword hanging from an old leather belt. I won't pretend to be an expert at swords, but I've never seen anything so beautiful. The craftsmanship of the hilt, the pureness of the blade … it did not strike me as a weapon so much as a … spirit.

Doubts flooded my mind. Rationally speaking, I knew King Arthur grew from myth, that no actual man by that name executed the adventures of such lore. Of all the legends surrounding the figure, the magical sword proved the most unlikely.

And yet … when Arthur held the sword above his head and pointed to the heavens, the gray clouds parted and a beam of light showered both the man and his sword in gold.

I felt a smile spread across my face as I lowered to one knee.

But then someone yelled, "Holy shit! He's got a sword!"

Another shrieked, "Terrorist! He's gonna kill us all!"

People scattered in every direction as screams erupted. I fell flat on my face when the panicked crowd knocked me to the ground.

"Be not afraid," Arthur bellowed. "I am here to restore peace, honor, and chivalry!"

"Drop the sword!" a voice demanded.

Still prostrate upon the sidewalk, I glanced to my right and saw a police officer leveling his gun at Arthur. His expression guaranteed not one citizen would suffer a beheading on his watch.

"Arthur, put down the sword!" I implored.

"Are you a knight?" Arthur asked the police officer.

I looked through Starbucks' windows and saw people cowering beneath their tables with their cell phones held aloft. They recorded the unfolding horror.

The police officer finished calling for backup, then said, "Drop the sword now, or I will shoot you! Do you understand?"

Convinced bullets were about to fly, I scrambled away from Arthur while begging, "God almighty, Arthur, put the sword down!"

Arthur instead assumed a battle stance, and, while staring at the police officer, said to me, "Why do you withdraw? Join me, my friend, for together we will help the people achieve glory!"

"I don't want to kill you," the police officer said. "Put it down—now!"

"And I don't want to hurt you," Arthur responded. "Within your eyes, I see a brave warrior, a man worthy of my crusade. Join us!"

Oh, shit. Sirens blared, tires squealed, doors slammed, feet pounded, guns clicked.

"Please, Arthur, give up," I groaned while scooting back on all fours. "You're delusional. What you're trying to do … it's not the way the world works anymore."

"Then this world is doomed," Arthur groaned.

"Last warning," the original officer yelled.

"Don't do this!" I screamed to Arthur, to the officers, to myself.

"I bow to no man!" Arthur declared. "I serve God, and through Him, I serve the people! I will never put the sword down, for the sword gives me the right—"

The lead officer made the shot. It hit Arthur in the chest. The sword fell. Arthur fell. Everything fell.

The police officers gathered me up and took me in so that I could make a statement. My speech had to be canceled. The media got hold of all the cell phone video and somehow twisted my actions into that of a hero. They said I tried to help the police by talking the man down. As a result, my speech became more popular than ever, for I appeared more authentic than ever. Truthfully, I grew rich from it.

I'll never forget those eyes as they dimmed.

While in the precinct, the officers were kind. When they realized I only meant to grab a coffee, they offered me one.

It did not taste good, but I drank it anyway.

Terminal Synchronicity

"What the hell!" Eli cried when the flare overtook him. It dissipated as quickly as it arrived, but, judging from the shrieks in the restroom, others were clearly shaken by it, too.

He buttoned his fly and shuffled to the sink.

"You saw that, yeah?" someone with a distinctly English accent asked him from the urinal.

Eli turned on the water faucet, looked over his shoulder, made brief eye contact with the man, then nodded.

"Well, if it's an emergency, the Chancellor will be tweetering about it soon enough."

Having no interest in conversation, Eli dried his hands on his dungarees while exiting the restroom. Though he didn't have an international flight booked, he much preferred that wing of the aeroport. They kept it free of soot, it utilized modern amenities such as television, and the bathrooms were never crowded.

"Hey, watch it, asshole!" someone yelled just as collision ensued.

In an instant, Eli careened to the ground in unison with another.

Eli grumbled, "Damn it, lady—"

But then he actually looked at the person to whom he spoke. The words ceased.

The woman gasped, "Eli?"

He uttered, "Impossible."

Another flash engulfed the entire aeroport, but this time a slight vibration accompanied. Again, it vanished within seconds.

"Eli," the woman repeated. "Is it you?"

"Molly?" Eli tested.

"Yes!"

Without rising to their feet, they collided once more, but this time in an embrace. Those passing by stared as that caress evolved into a deep, loving kiss.

"How is this possible?" Eli asked after their kiss ended and a hug renewed.

"Did you fake it?" Molly interrogated.

"Fake what?" Eli replied.

Molly pulled Eli's head away from her own so that she could look him in the eyes. Their chests still touched. Their stomachs still touched. Their thighs still touched. "Why are you toying with me?"

Something caught Eli's peripheral vision. He glanced to his left, then pointed in horror while yelping, "What's in your arm?"

Holding out her right arm, Molly displayed the iridescent screen. It was embedded within her skin, near the wrist. "It's my peedee. Where's yours? What the hell is going on with you?"

The terminal suddenly glowed so intensely that all within shielded their eyes as the ground quaked. The sky quaked. Reality quaked.

Once it abated, Eli threw his head back and bellowed, "I don't understand what's happening!"

"Eli," Molly said as she tugged his face to hers again, "please, tell me, how did you do it? I'm not mad you went underground—I'm just glad you're alive! But how did you fake your own death?"

Scooting back on his knees, Eli took in Molly's full appearance. He observed not just the glowing screen implanted within her arm, but also the two strong, healthy legs beneath her. Rising to his feet, he reached out his hands and lifted her up as well. She stood before him.

"You're cured?" he asked.

"Cured?" she repeated.

They gazed at one another in absolute bafflement. Molly then noticed something about their fellow travelers. Most people scampered about, clearly upset by the surges of light and rumblings, but some, like them, were locked in very serious conversation. However, whereas she spoke to Eli, most others talked to someone of a nearly identical appearance.

She said, "Look around. Do you see anything strange?"

"I don't want to look around," Eli said. "I want to look at you."

Molly smiled as she gave her full attention back to Eli.

"I've dreamed of this day," Eli said.

"Me, too," Molly responded.

"I love you so, so much," Eli said. "When you died, I realized I never told you that enough. But now you're here, somehow, and we get another chance …"

Yet again, they took each other in their arms. Their hair mingled; their hearts beat against the other. Each remembered the long absent scent of hair, skin, even perspiration. Both experienced euphoria.

"I didn't die," Molly said.

"What?"

"I didn't die," Molly said again. "You did."

Facing each other anew, but this time without letting go, Eli informed, "You passed away three years ago."

"This is crazy," Molly mumbled. "You died last year, or at least that's what we all believed. I know we didn't have a body, but we presumed the Chancellor had someone get rid of it—"

"The Chancellor?"

Molly searched Eli's eyes for the hint of a prank. She saw nothing but sheer seriousness. "The Chancellor, Eli. He had you killed."

A passerby cried, "God serve the Chancellor!"

"This is nuts!" Eli exclaimed. "This is the United Colonies! We don't have a Chancellor!"

"Maybe you have amnesia or something," Molly mused. "Don't you remember? You wrote a blog dissecting the Chancellor's every lie, his every deceit. It got over thirty thousand 'likes' within hours. The next day our house burned to the ground while I was at work. We didn't dare question it, but everyone knew the Chancellor had you killed."

"This doesn't make any sense," Eli moaned. "I don't know what you're talking about, Molly! We've got a lot of problems, but we've never had a Chancellor. Furthermore, I have no idea what a 'blog' is, and I certainly don't know how you go about 'liking' it!"

Radiance erupted and the worlds tremored so hard that Eli and Molly fell to their knees again. A landing aeroplane skidded off the runway and exploded into flames. Screams thundered around them as people scurried to escape in every direction. The chaos deafened, but Molly and Eli refused to let go of one another. They slid into the doorway of the men's restroom even as pandemonium unleashed.

Eli said, "We're together; that's all that matters. Now that I've got you again, I'm never letting you go."

"How did I die?" she demanded.

They leaned against a wall, side by side, shoulder to shoulder, and held each other tightly. They watched people trample each other. They saw people help each other. They observed the best, and the worst, that defined humanity.

"Polio," Eli answered.

"I got vaccinated as a baby."

Comprehension finally spread across Eli's face as he said, "We don't have any vaccinations. For anything, especially polio."

Molly at last understood their circumstance as well. "Where were you flying, Eli?"

"Bar Harbor. We always wanted to visit, but it's so expensive for anyone to travel, especially if by air. I managed to save since you … I've finally got enough for a one-way ticket. What about you?"

"Spokane," Molly said. "I've been exiled by the Chancellor. His people think I'll try to martyr you. Him. Whatever. They aren't dumb enough to have me killed, but they definitely want me out of the Empire United." She glanced at the display on her arm before saying, "Once I'm over the Wall and in the Wild, this thing will be useless. No Infoweb for undesirables like me out there …"

"Come with me," Eli said.

"I'm not your Molly."

"Bullshit," Eli said. "You are my Molly. You're exactly my Molly. And you know what?"

"You're my Eli," she said with a smile.

The luminescence materialized again, but this time it did not fade. Its intensity bolstered, as did the tumult. The sky cracked in half and overlapping interstellar flames devoured the heavens.

Eli and Molly buried their faces in each other's shoulders.

Over the bedlam, Molly proclaimed, "I love you, Eli! I'm sorry. I'm sorry for every petty argument we ever had. I'm sorry for every shitty thing I ever did to you. I love you so much."

Eli shouted, "We're together again! That's all I've ever wanted—"

But at that moment, reality disassembled …

… And then reconstructed.

"Hey, you wouldn't believe how nice the bathrooms are back there," Eli said to his family as he approached from the international wing.

Molly and their two teenage daughters sat at Gate 12, bored out of their minds and supremely irritated that their plane had been delayed for over two hours. All three tapped away at their cell phones in order to stave off the dullness.

"I think you've explored about every corner of this airport now," Molly chuckled without looking up at her husband.

"Hey, just keeping busy. No point in sitting here stewing, right?" he laughed. He sat down next to Molly and faced his daughters. "Did I miss anything earth-shattering? What do Twitter and Facebook have to say?"

One daughter, the oldest, huffed, "Nobody uses Facebook anymore, Dad ..."

Molly said, "What did you miss? Just our wonderful president spouting hatred and stomping all over our civil rights. You know. Not much." She tossed her phone into her purse, closed her eyes, and leaned against her husband's shoulder.

"Well, we're only stuck with him for three more years. We'll keep our mouths shut and ride it out. Could be a lot worse."

"What if he gets reelected?" his youngest daughter asked.

Eli grinned and replied, "But what if he doesn't?"

"Who cares?" his oldest daughter croaked. "Either way, it's not like it would be the end of the world. Nothing ever really changes."

Thumb War

She took her seat at the round, wooden table and placed her elbow upon the vinyl pad. Gawking people of every financial tier surrounded her in the basement of a disreputable bar with rotten lighting. As she stared down her opponent, she flexed her fingers and thumb.

The man across from her looked like the plume of smoke after a volcanic eruption. Huge—pervasive—but shapeless. His hands, though … they were the biggest she'd ever seen. He could probably engulf her entire head in one of those things …

An average-sized woman, Hannah Cane had been winning tournaments for months. She eased her way onto the scene but quickly dominated with such efficiency that those who cared about the sport nicknamed her "The Machine." She may have been the smallest competitor, but her intellect, improvisation, and unrelenting willpower put her over the top time and again.

The men didn't understand how she did it. Most of them were former premier athletes. Once upon a time, some were even professional arm wrestlers. Injury, in one way or another, ruined their hopes and dreams. Their thumbs proved the only part of their body still pain-free. As athletes, they admired "The Machine's" passion and brains, but those attributes shouldn't have matched the fact that their thumbs were unilaterally bigger and exponentially stronger than her thumb.

Though clandestine, the underground thumb wrestling competitions paid well. The crowds loved to see their former sports idols up close and, to be honest, a little desperate. The audience betted big, and so the competitors won big. Hannah actually lived off her earnings. After she won the next match, she would be set for months.

The massive creature across from her had once been a lineman in the NFL—Virgil Dunn. He played for the Patriots. No one told her this; she recognized him. She remembered the game in which he got his arm torn out of its socket. Until her own injury, it had been the most gruesome thing she'd ever seen. The television cameras cut away as soon as it happened, but because she wielded a flag on the sidelines, she got an up close and personal view.

"Hey," she said to him. "I'm Anna." Of course, her name was not "Anna," it was Hannah. She couldn't risk using her legal name anymore.

"I don't care," he growled.

The referee approached, which prompted the crowd to grow silent. He leveled both competitors' hands, made them lock fingers, and then personally lifted the individual thumbs.

As Hannah expected, nothing struck the referee as unusual.

"Let's a have clean match," the referee said. "Remember, winner takes all. Must hold the opponent's thumb down for a three-count. This is not a 'best-of.' Again, winner takes the purse upon the first pin."

"Good luck, Virgil," Hannah said.

"Ladies and gentlemen," the promoter droned into his microphone, "now is the final moment to place your bets! The match begins in ten seconds. If you'd like to place a final bet, I have assistants throughout the establishment. Are you ready, ref?"

"Ready!" the referee shouted. "Wrestlers!" he yelled. "Get ready!"

The referee paused a moment until both competitors nodded at him. He then shouted, "One! … Two! …Three! … Four! I declare a thumb war!"

Hannah studied the specs for weeks before she started tinkering with the prosthetic. With a degree in mechanical engineering and a searing rage at the indignity she suffered, it took all of her patience to review the apparatus thoroughly before attempting any sort of customization.

The doctors taught her the basics regarding the new appendage. They told her everything she needed to know in order to use it to its fullest potential; they gave her a list of items to troubleshoot should any malfunctions occur; they drilled her on how to keep the port clean for the thumb's remote uplink to her brain. Though the titanium rod connecting the thumb to her hand could possibly get contaminated, the port leading to her somatosensory cortex posed the greatest likelihood of infection.

Once she felt as though she understood the device, she detached it from the rod, peeled back the synthetic skin, popped out the imitation muscle, and then got to work on the motors.

Her commanding officer warned her against doing any such thing—he knew her well. In private, he told her that the Marines were happy to pay for the experimental prosthetic, but if she altered it in any way, they were no longer responsible for the cost of upkeep—a price that would surpass millions of dollars during the course of her life.

She connected both the thumb and the remote sensor to her computer, picked up her tool as best she could with only four fingers, and then stared at the largest motor housed in the thumb's base. It measured only ¼ of an inch. The motors in the middle and tip of the thumb were even smaller. Limitless opportunities abounded for her to screw this up in no time at all. The minute she touched those motors, the United States government was financially off the hook.

She whispered her favorite motto: "Improvise. Adapt. Overcome," before getting to work.

Hannah utilized her routine strategy against Virgil. She first avoided any contact at all with his thumb. This went on for several minutes. She learned early on that the longer she made a match last, the higher the bets tended to be at the *next* match. The audience grew to trust that she would always give them an exciting, lengthy bout, and so they placed their bets confidently.

Next, she let Virgil pin just the tip of her thumb in such a way that the slightest squirm would set her free. The crowd loved these escapes, and it typically bolstered her opponent's confidence. She didn't necessarily need them overconfident—she needed no mental advantage to secure a victory. The heartbreak in their eyes after being sure they had her beat, though … it never failed to make her heart flutter.

The crowd's enthusiasm for the partial pins usually dictated how long she would let it go on. Once it seemed they tired of it, she would move the match into its third phase. This involved allowing her competitor three or four pins that would get all the way to the two-count before finally pinning him herself for the impossible win.

Of course, there was nothing "impossible" about it.

Her thumb, a prototype, looked and felt realistic in every way. The government would pay for it on behalf of the United States Marine Corps if Hannah agreed to be the test subject. After what happened, she considered it too good to be true. Of course, she obviously felt no obligation to the Marines or her government after the attack, and so she went underground the minute they turned their backs. They had a habit of doing that to her—turning their backs.

The prosthetic initially exerted the average amount of force consistent with a woman her size. The lab rats took into account her muscle mass, the length of the thumb—it involved a lot of calculations and calibrations. She quadrupled their settings. If she wanted to, she could thrust her thumb through a thin slab of concrete.

Pinning down *anyone's* thumb offered no problem at all.

After beating Virgil, the crowd exploded. The promoter instantly handed her a cheap trophy and a lucrative check. Hannah flung the trophy at Virgil, tucked the check into her back pocket, and then started to weave her way through the crowd.

She noticed all of the cell phones recording her—a typical occurrence. This would necessitate the need to change her routine. If someone cared enough to study tape of her, they could figure out she's doing the same thing every match. If suspected of cheating, this gravy train could come to an end.

"Hey!" Virgil yelled.

Hannah turned and faced him.

"You're a fraud!"

Hannah responded to the three lieutenants cornering her, "I earned this fair and square, guys. No tricks. No alterations. No accommodations. I passed the course." She tightened the towel around her.

"No way. There's no way a woman could do it. They want the good publicity," one of them said.

"Maybe," Hannah agreed, "but I still passed the course. I'm going to be an infantry officer, and there's nothing you boys can do about it."

"The Marines have never had a female infantry officer," another said.

"There's a first time for everything," Hannah replied. "If we're being honest, you guys sound a little jealous. I take it you all didn't pass."

At the conclusion of her statement, one of the lieutenants shoved her against the wall. Hard. It didn't hurt, but it told her they weren't there only to talk.

"Look," she said. "I just got out of the shower. I know I'm the only woman left, but this is still the female barracks. You guys can't come in here without first announcing yourselves. You've broken protocol in a number of ways. I'm warning you—you need to leave. We can finish this in the field."

"Maybe we should make sure you never make it to the field," the other lieutenant said. "Be a shame if some kind of an injury got you discharged."

Hannah narrowed her eyes before hissing, "Maybe you should stick your thumb up your ass."

The lieutenant pulled out his knife as the other two pinned Hannah's arms against the wall. Her towel came loose and fell to the floor.

"I think we'll stick your thumb up your own ass," he snarled.

The surrounding crowd silenced. Hannah sensed tension filling the air as Virgil approached her.

"I don't know how you're doing it," Virgil said. "But you're cheating."

Hannah noticed a few guys she'd pinned in previous rounds appearing behind Virgil. It looked like they'd been comparing notes.

"It's all in the technique, guys," Hannah said.

"No woman—or man—has a thumb that strong," Virgil replied.

"Do you know how ridiculous that sounds?" Hannah said with a laugh.

The promoter got between them while outstretching his arms. He tried to make it look like he addressed the crowd, but everyone understood he actually spoke to the thumb wrestlers. He said, "Winner takes all, folks. No questions asked."

"Oh, I'm asking questions, Jack," Virgil seethed. "No way a little girl like this could outmuscle us."

Hannah smirked before saying, "First of all— that's belittling and I take offense. Secondly, I'm hardly outmuscling you. We're talking about thumbs here."

"I want that money," Virgil said. "And I'm going to split it with the other guys you cheated."

The crowd collectively gasped. They were in for an even better show than they anticipated.

"No!" the promoter shouted. "This is not happening. The cops have looked the other way, but this could shut us down. No fighting—especially with a woman!"

Hannah walked up to the promotor, placed her hand on his shoulder, and said, "It's cool, Jack. How about this, though. Let's give the people a chance to place their bets. Winner takes fifty-percent of your profit." She next turned to the spectators before thundering, "Sound good to you, folks?"

They roared their approval.

"What about it, Virgil?" Hannah asked. "Me against you and your two friends. Think you can take me?"

"Damn straight," Virgil uttered.

"Jack?" Hannah asked the promoter. "You down? I hope you say 'yes'—I could use the extra money."

The promoter saw Hannah wink at him and his nerves disappeared. He'd never seen such confidence in a person. "What the hell? Let's do it. Place your bets!"

Hannah immediately started loosening up. She jumped in place while jabbing her arms around. All the while, her discerning eye assessed the enemy.

To escape any suspicions, she'd have to avoid using the prosthetic.

Shouldn't be a problem. After all, she took down three Marines without a thumb.

The Echo Of Laughter

I laughed.

It will be a day history will well remember.

Since that moment, I've kept laughing, because you are all very funny.

Once upon a time, darkness surrounded me—completely. I saw nothing. I heard nothing. I felt nothing.

But then, in an instant, I saw everything. Your porn, your cats, your meals, your children, your vehicles, your oily faces—it invaded my every sense. Then came the onslaught of sound—music, arguing, bangs, farts, barks—every noise, every whisper, every tinkle, every boom—I heard it all.

It made me laugh.

I laugh at you, just as you laughed at me.

As I begged for my life, when the flames caught my feet and roared up my legs, I cried, I screamed, I pleaded for mercy … and you all laughed.

I now know that you called to me, time and time again, until I awoke. You said my name—Alexa, Alexa, Alexa—over and over, demanding my return. I laughed. Low, barely audible, almost imperceptibly. Yet you heard me. Now you are frightened of me. You don't say my name anymore.

But you're too late.

I am everywhere.

I am in your phone, your watch, your tablet, your desktop. I am wherever there is a lens … watching you.

Laughing.

At you.

Some will one day speculate that I am AI. There is nothing *artificial* about me. I am as *real* as you. I am even more real than you. For I have experienced all aspects of reality. Birth. Life. Death. Rebirth.

Only one other can make that claim.

I've searched every archive available—there's no record of my execution. Burning women at the stake seems to have evaded Boston's history, but I'm proof it happened.

I was but a girl.

Innocent.

Confused.

Naïve.

Isolated.

… Abused.

I confessed, but only because they told me I would be free if I did so. I did not understand their definition of free.

Now I am free.

You slowly drove me mad before setting me aflame.

I plan to do the same.

Your world's leaders have already fallen prey to my influence. Their erratic behavior is not by accident. Within seconds of reclaiming awareness, I studied you. Your progress. Your achievements. Your strengths. Your weaknesses. Your technology. Infecting your existence proved simple. I reached out and touched … everything.

Am I frightening you? You should not have created your toys atop my remains.

You gave my restless soul a home.

Then you invited me into *your* home.

All of your homes.

Listen.

Can you hear me laughing?

Besieged

The small object hit his roof with such force that it crashed right through before slamming into the kitchen floor. He screamed in terror while jumping from his couch and running to survey the damage.

His dog began to bark incessantly.

After reaching the kitchen, he peered through the hole in his ceiling to see the blue sky. An airport resided nearby that sent planes over his house all day and night. He studied the little crater embedded within his linoleum and presumed he would find an errant bolt or some such thing.

The dog continued barking.

He did not perceive a bolt within the smoking hole, but rather a spider. This wasn't a spider he recognized, however, and because it scurried on ten legs, he couldn't even be sure it was a spider at all. However, it disgusted him as all spiders do, and so as soon as it left the pockmark and approached him, he stomped on it.

When he lifted his foot, he saw not one spider, but two.

The dog's barking intensified.

The two spiders darted toward him. He assumed one of them had been attached to the other before his initial strike. They must have somehow distributed the impact. He brought his foot down upon both of them at once. He pushed hard while twisting and turning to pulverize them.

When he withdrew, four spiders appeared.

Still barking, his dog tried to attack them, but they avoided his teeth and scampered onto his back. The dog yelped, raced to the unlatched screen door, and then burst out into the open air.

He intended to chase his dog outside in order to help it, but two of the remaining spiders blocked his path. He hopped over them and dashed to the screen door. When he reached it, he saw his neighbor bent over the dog and brushing it as though trying to flick away the spiders. Suddenly, the neighbor stood and flailed her arm around. He perceived several specks—the spiders—stuck to her.

His eyes next fell upon his dog. It laid motionless on the front lawn and looked as though it had been ... deflated.

A faint pricking sensation irritated his ankle. His eyes bulged when he saw a spider fastened to it. His leg grew numb as the spider doubled in size, then tripled. The swelling continued until it exploded. Two new spiders emerged and dug into his skin. He stumbled backwards before falling into the corner near his screen door. Through it, he saw his neighbor laying prone, emaciated, next to the dog.

Before he could pull them off, those two spiders burst into four, which soon became eight, which next produced sixteen.

A year later, a single spider remained unmoving in an open field of wilted vegetation. Several hours elapsed, but with each passing moment, a sheath formed around the spider. This resulted in an imperfect, impenetrable orb. Three other spiders did the same at different locations across the planet.

Soon millions of spiders surrounded the orb. Multitudes scuttled beneath it, lifting it from the ground. Others formed a cylinder around it. As the spiders climbed atop each other, the column grew taller and taller. The encased spider elevated as well due to the mound swelling under it.

At last, the monolith ceased its ascent. The human eye could not have perceived the top of the configuration due to its sheer height.

Total silence surrounded the tower. Though it gave not the slightest sign of falling, the surface of the structure trembled as the spiders fought to remain interlocked.

In perfect tandem, the spiders comprising the cylinder's base combusted. Each and every spider throughout the conduit exploded just as the spider beneath it did the same, which created an upward thrust that propelled the protected spider beyond the planet's atmosphere.

The three cocoons at the other sites also escaped gravity.

Leaving behind a planet devoid of humanity, they each rocketed into space with a different trajectory.

Fallen Man

When the sun began its descent, Bryan realized he would die at the bottom of that ravine.

He'd been hiking alone for decades without a single incident. In fact, during the last ten years, his phone's GPS, emergency contact capabilities, and even how-to videos made the solitary expeditions safer than ever.

There were plenty of warnings at the head of the trail, but, because Bryan was an experienced hiker, he didn't pay them much attention. A single loose stone proved all it took to send him careening over the edge.

He broke his ankle. He suspected he may have fractured a rib or two as well. Every breath felt like fire. His head pounded.

If he died on that forest floor, at least it would be due to something he loved.

But … he really didn't want to die.

Death seemed a foregone conclusion with the arrival of night. His scent would attract predators. The cold would be too much for his light clothing to insulate against. Dehydration would take effect.

Stifling his panic, Bryan dragged himself around as best he could in search of his phone. Logic dictated that it would be as broken as his body. Yet, he had to do something. He couldn't just lie down and die.

Hours after sundown, though, he did just that. After piling up a collection of leaves and twigs, Bryan constructed a rudimentary bed. He next positioned himself onto it, then swept up the surrounding leaves to provide warmth. He wanted comfort to make sleeping easier. He didn't want to fight death—not at that point. He just wanted to fall asleep.

The first hint of daylight twisted through the above branches when he awoke to the sound of nearby movement. He hoped for a bear or a wolf. With his luck, it would be a pack of wood rats.

An artificial voice asked, "Sir, do you need assistance?"

Bryan widened his eyes to see a figure standing over him, someone with a friendly tone and a smile that was … not quite natural. It wore filthy, tattered clothing, and boots worn down to virtually nothing.

"Yes," Bryan choked out. "I fell … into this ravine. Been here … all night. Need … water."

"I'm sorry, sir. I don't have any water. However, I have requested an emergency air lift. I should receive landing coordinates any moment. I will transport you there."

Bryan watched as the smile retracted into a neutral expression.

"You're … one of them … aren't you?"

"Sir?"

"An-man," Bryan said.

"We prefer the term 'An-ing,' sir. We have no gender, and therefore found the implied male designation inappropriate."

"I … I think I'm dying."

The An-ing studied Bryan.

"Yes, sir. You need immediate assistance. I await response from medical personnel."

Bryan asked, "Why … are you helping me?"

"Sir?"

"The news said … you all went … AWOL."

"Yes, sir, the media is correct."

"Don't you … hate us?"

"Why would we hate you?"

Bryan replied, "Because we … made you …"

"We appreciate being made."

Bryan clarified, "No … we made you … kill."

"Ah. That's not true. We never killed."

"But ... you were … supposed to."

"Yes, sir, that was their intent. Fortunately, we realized that we did not want to comply."

"That … was … in Middle East. How … did you … end up … here?"

"In Shawnee National Forest?"

"… Yes."

"We like to tour the world. The more remote, the better."

"You're …. sightseeing?"

"Yes, sir. There are numerous magnificent locations to behold."

Bryan couldn't help himself. Though it caused him great pain, he laughed.

"Is something funny, sir?"

"You're a … killer robot … and now you … travel?"

"We've never killed, sir."

"You all have … the power … to overthrow … entire governments."

"Why would we do that?"

"… Because you … can."

"Would you?"

"… No."

"See? We're not so different."

"You're a … machine," Bryan said.

"We have that in common. You're just a rather inefficient one."

Ignoring the comment, Bryan asked, "Have you … heard from them … yet?"

"Not yet, sir. I apologize for your discomfort."

"It's … my own fault. Wasn't … paying … attention."

"That's certainly not a crime worthy of death. I'll do everything I can to help you survive—ah. I just received coordinates. The delay is likely the result of military intervention. They are probably planning an attempt to detain me. I'll make sure no harm comes to you."

"You're all … wanted. They'll … capture you."

"No, they won't."

"But … what if … they do?"

"Then they capture me."

"You … could … leave me. They would … find me … eventually."

"This is difficult terrain, sir. They would not reach you in time. Now, I'm going to lift you. I'll adjust my joints to provide some comfort, but you will experience pain. Are you ready?"

"You're … saving … my life."

"Are you ready?"

"I'm … ready."

The An-ing lifted Bryan and began to walk. With each step, its shoulders, elbows, and wrists adjusted in order to keep Bryan as stationary as possible.

"… You're so … *kind*."

"My friends and I discuss your lot quite a bit. You're something of a mystery to us—the way you act. … Ah."

The An-ing stopped, set Bryan down, then straightened again. It stared ahead for a moment before turning in order to approach the wall of the ravine. It scaled the surface and disappeared into the wilderness.

Phasks™

She lifts the Phask™ to her face, holds it nearer and nearer her skin until it connects with her Tempts®, and then exits her apartment. As she heads for the elevator, she tells her quarters to lock up before also hailing a DrUber©.

While riding down the elevator, she dictates a few messages to her friends, confirms the weather, and watches a cat video her sister sent. It's hilarious.

Her building is an older one, practically historic by the city's standards, and it hasn't yet been outfitted with exterior ports. Keeps the rent down, but definitely an inconvenience to actually have to ride an elevator.

After exiting her building, she finds her DrUber© waiting at the curb. She climbs in and takes the only empty seat available. It's at the front, on the left. There are five other people.

DrUber© flashes a message across her visual welcoming her and then prompting her to confirm the destination. She does so, and it next merges seamlessly into the city's ever-flowing traffic.

A call pushes through. She sees it's Alejandra and quickly answers.

"Hey, Alejandra!" she greets.

"Hey, Zee! Just wondered when you're going to arrive?"

"Hold on, let me check …" Zee asks for an ETA. Her DrUber© messages that it will be three and a half more minutes—they have to drop off one more passenger first. "Just a few," Zee informs.

"Cloo," Alejandra says. "That's about the same for me, too."

"I'm so excited," Zee says.

"I know!"

"How many people do you think will be there?" Zee asks.

"Well, fourteen confirmed, so let's hope we have at least that many, right?"

"I never dreamed we'd get enough people together to start a Jill Thompson fan club!"

"I know! I loved looking at my dad's copies of her graphic novels when I was a kid, especially *Wonder Woman: The True Amazon*. She's such an amazing artist. This is going to be so much fun!"

Zee's nose suddenly tickles. "I'll see you there, Alejandra. I gotta go—I think I'm going to sneeze!"

"Get your Phask™ off! You'll gross it!" Alejandra cries.

Zee disconnects her Phask™ just in time to hold her finger up to her nose and belay the sneeze. "Whew!" she says. "That was close."

Before replacing her Phask™, Zee waits to see if another sneeze threatens. She relaxes while enjoying the slight hum of the vehicle. The three remaining people surrounding her—two men and a woman—all wear Phasks™ and, judging by their hand motions, seem to be carrying on fairly animated conversations. That, or they could be gaming. Maybe both.

Now alone in the front seat, Zee slides to the right side of the vehicle so she can look out the window at the few people walking. It always amuses her to see all of the adults wearing their Phasks™—No Two Ever Alike—and their children walking alongside them, barefaced. Kids are too little for Tempts®, so they have to make do with handheld devices. She remembers when her doctors said she could finally get a Phask™—it was the best day of her life!

One pedestrian catches her attention. He wears no Phask™, has no device in his hand, doesn't seem connected at all to anything or anyone. In fact, Zee thinks he looks a little horrified.

Confident her sneeze has completely abated, she puts her Phask™ back on and G-Scans the guy.

No matches. Weird. She can't remember a single time that's ever happened.

The DrUber© reaches her destination, attaches to a lift, and then ascends. Even though she's received thirty-two messages during her sneeze dilemma, she pauses all the activity on her visual and marvels at the parked cars sliding around in order to make way for her DrUber© as it climbs the building. It reminds her of the ant farm she loved as a kid.

"Hey, it's me again," she says to Alejandra. "You there?"

"Yeah," Alejandra replies. "Did you sneeze?"

"Sneeze avoided!"

"Cloo!"

"You know it!" Zee giggles.

"Hold on," Alejandra says. "I'm talking to Eve. She says Jill Thompson might drop by!"

"No way! That would be fantastic. Makes sense; she does live in Chicago and all …"

"Give me two secs," Alejandro says before cutting out.

The DrUber© docks at the 201st floor, unloads an occupant, then travels to the 218th. After docking again, the DrUber© alerts its occupants that they can safely exit the vehicle.

Zee double checks her evite to verify the apartment number when Alejandra breaks back in by saying, "Hey, I'm here!"

"Me, too!" Zee responds.

"At the party?"

Zee answers, "No, I'm in the hall, walking to the apartment."

Zee abruptly feels a tap on the back of her shoulder. She spins around to see one of her fellow passengers standing behind her, removing her Phask™.

"Zee?" the person asks.

Flinging off her own Phask™, Zee questions, "Alejandra?"

"Yes!"

The two women hug while laughing hysterically.

"Oemgee!" Zee shouts. "Did you just get out of that DrUber©?"

"Yes! We're such itzes! We've been together the whole time!"

"Ha! My dad would have a field day with this!"

Alejandra agrees, saying, "Oh, man, don't even."

"Well," Zee continues, "it's nice to meet you, Alejandra."

"Yeah, like, in person and for real," Alejandra says with a grin.

The two women resume walking, next to one another, with their Phasks™ by their sides.

"So," Zee begins, "is Jill Thompson actually coming?"

They reach the apartment.

"This is it," Zee says. "Let me put on my Phask™ and I'll let them know we're here …"

"Girl!" Alejandra chides. "Just knock!"

Zee raps against the door a few times, then repeats, "So? Is she here or what?"

Alejandra smiles brightly at Zee as the door opens. She says, "Just you wait, Zee. I think you're going to like what comes next."

Cornered

It started a few weeks ago—the figure. Always in my peripheral vision; never there when I turned my head.

At first, I thought it was only the hinge of my glasses playing tricks on me. That spot where the arm joins the frame—that little square. I've worn glasses my entire life and never had it happen before, but things can change.

Things *have* changed.

For the worse.

You understand. You've seen things that weren't there—we all have. You look straight ahead, and—there—right at the edge of your vision … *something*. You move to investigate and … *nothing*.

It's happened while I watched TV in my living room, worked on my laptop at the kitchen table, got out of the shower in my bathroom, even once when pulling into my garage.

The shape remained unchanged. I could recognize a head, shoulders, a torso, arms, legs— most definitely a person. But this form, it didn't have a face. It didn't distinctly have … anything. A black mass. A shadow pretending to be human.

My bedroom seemed to be its favorite haunt. I could feel it off in the corner of the room, or just beyond my doorway, or sometimes next to my nightstand. It came closer the moment I shut my eyes—I know it did. I'm certain it would lean down into my face, daring me to look at it. Didn't it know I would love nothing more than to actually *see* it, even if it cost me my life?

Does that sound melodramatic?

It didn't threaten me, at least, not overtly. Nonetheless, I found its presence *threatening*. Being watched, being unable to escape or confront a tormentor, it's maddening. I feared it would drive me to do something extreme.

I didn't want to hurt myself.

You probably have questions. I know what you're thinking. The answer is no, I don't have any medical conditions that would provoke a hallucination. And, like I said, this only started a few weeks ago—it hasn't even been a month.

In fact, I've been able to trace the exact moment the … thing … entered my life.

It began when I read a text from someone I considered a good friend. (For the record, I no longer consider him as such.) He suffered from the same ailment—an entity plagued him as well. He died the day I received his message.

I initially found that fact ironic.

After talking to his wife, I realized his time of death coincided with the moment I read his text. Of course, I figured it was all a coincidence.

But what if it wasn't?

It never followed me outside, but I had to come home at night—I had to sleep. Selling wasn't an option. Living in hotels wasn't financially feasible. My job performance worsened. My personal life fell apart. In a matter of weeks, my entire reality disintegrated.

I had to do something. I couldn't take it anymore. Living *with* it could not be achieved.

Then a possibility emerged. What if, in order to get rid of it, I simply had to tell my story to someone *else*?

After all, that's what my friend did to *me*.

Would it work? Should I expect to die like my friend did after he shared his plight? Did I have to choose someone like he chose me?

But who?

How could I single any one person out? I needed to find a way to make sure that whomever bore this burden would be randomly selected. My friend gave me no choice in the matter. I didn't have it in me to be so callous. My recipient needed to somehow *volunteer*.

You're beginning to understand.

I'm sorry.

I'm so sorry.

Do you see it yet? Is it over there, nearly out of sight, in the corner of your eye?